C000100349

WOMEN HATE
TILL DEATH

THE CLASSIC HANK JANSON

The first original Hank Janson book appeared in 1946, and the last in 1971. However, the classic era on which we are focusing in the Telos reissue series lasted from 1946 to 1953.

The following is a checklist of those books, which were subdivided into five main series and a number of "specials".

The titles so far reissued by Telos are indicated by way of an asterisk.

Pre-series books

When Dames Get Tough (1946)
Scarred Faces (1946)

Series One

1   This Woman Is Death (1948)
2   Lady, Mind That Corpse (1948)
3   Gun Moll For Hire (1948)
4   No Regrets For Clara (1949)
5   Smart Girls Don't Talk (1949)
6   Lilies For My Lovely (1949)
7   Blonde On The Spot (1949)
8   Honey, Take My Gun (1949)
9   Sweetheart, Here's Your Grave (1949)
10 Gunsmoke In Her Eyes (1949)
11 Angel, Shoot To Kill (1949)
12 Slay-Ride For Cutie (1949)

Series Two

13 Sister, Don't Hate Me (1949)
14 Some Look Better Dead (1950)
15 Sweetie, Hold Me Tight (1950)
16 Torment For Trixie (1950)
17 Don't Dare Me, Sugar (1950)
18 The Lady Has A Scar (1950)
19 The Jane With The Green Eyes (1950)
20 Lola Brought Her Wreath (1950)
21 Lady, Toll The Bell (1950)
22 The Bride Wore Weeds (1950)
23 Don't Mourn Me Toots (1951)
24 This Dame Dies Soon (1951)

Series Three

25 Baby, Don't Dare Squeal (1951)
26 Death Wore A Petticoat (1951)

27 Hotsy, You'll Be Chilled (1951)
28 It's Always Eve That Weeps (1951)
29 Frails Can Be So Tough (1951)
30 Milady Took The Rap (1951)
31 Women Hate Till Death (1951) *
32 Broads Don't Scare Easy (1951)
33 Skirts Bring Me Sorrow (1951)
34 Sadie Don't Cry Now (1952)
35 The Filly Wore A Rod (1952)
36 Kill Her If You Can (1952)

Series Four

37 Murder (1952)
38 Conflict (1952)
39 Tension (1952)
40 Whiplash (1952)
41 Accused (1952)
42 Killer (1952)
43 Suspense (1952)
44 Pursuit (1953)
45 Vengeance (1953)
46 Torment (1953) *
47 Amok (1953)
48 Corruption (1953)

Series Five

49 Silken Menace (1953)
50 Nyloned Avenger (1953)

Specials

A   Auctioned (1952)
B   Persian Pride (1952)
C   Desert Fury (1953)
D   Unseen Assassin (1953)
E   One Man In His Time (1953)
F   Deadly Mission (1953)

WOMEN
HATE
TILL
DEATH

by

HANK
JANSON

This edition first published in England in 2003
by Telos Publishing Ltd
61 Elgar Avenue, Tolworth, Surrey, KT5 9JP, England
www.telos.co.uk

Telos Publishing Ltd values feedback.
Please e-mail us with any comments you may have
about this book to: feedback@telos.co.uk

ISBN: 1-903889-81-2
This edition © 2003 Telos Publishing Ltd
Introduction © 2003 Steve Holland.

Novel by Stephen D Frances
Cover by Reginald Heade
With thanks to Steve Holland
www.hankjanson.co.uk
Silhouette device by Philip Mendoza
Cover design by David J Howe
This edition prepared for publication by Stephen James Walker
Internal design, typesetting and layout by David Brunt

The Hank Janson name, logo and silhouette device
are trademarks of Telos Publishing Ltd

First published in England by New Fiction Press, October 1951

Printed in England by
Antony Rowe Ltd, Bumper's Farm Industrial Estate,
Chippenham, Wiltshire, SN14 6LH

1 2 3 4 5 6 7 8 9 10 11 12 13 14 15

British Library Cataloguing in Publication Data. A catalogue
record for this book is available from the British Library.

PUBLISHER'S NOTE

The appeal of the Hank Janson books to a modern readership lies not only in the quality of the storytelling, which is as powerfully compelling today as it was when they were first published, but also in the fascinating insight they afford into the attitudes, customs, modes of expression and, significantly, morals of the 1940s and 1950s. That is perhaps all the more important with a book like *Women Hate Till Death*, when one realises that its harrowing descriptions of life in a Nazi concentration camp were written less than six years after the end of World War II. Whereas now such things are the stuff of history books, back then they would have been fresh and immediate in readers' minds.

We have therefore endeavoured to make *Women Hate Till Death*, and all our other Hank Janson reissues, as faithful to the original edition as possible. Unlike some other publishers who, when reissuing vintage fiction, have been known to make editorial changes to remove aspects that might offend present-day sensibilities, we have left the original narrative absolutely intact. So if, in the original edition, Hank made, say, a casually sexist remark to the effect that most women are bad drivers - as he does in *Women Hate Till Death* - then that is what you will read in the Telos edition as well.

That's just the kinda guy Hank was.

Which brings us to a point about language. The original editions of these classic Hank Janson titles made quite frequent use of phonetic "Americanisms" such as "kinda", "gotta", "wanna" and so on. Again, we have left these unchanged in the Telos reissues, to give readers as genuine as possible a taste of what it was like to read these books when they first came out, even though such devices have since become sorta out of fashion.

The only way in which we have amended the original text has been to correct obvious lapses in spelling, grammar and punctuation - we have, for instance, added question marks in the not-infrequent cases where they were omitted from the ends of questions in the original - and to remedy clear typesetting errors. So, for instance, the Telos edition of *Women Hate Till Death* has only one chapter headed Chapter Nine, whereas the original had two!

Lastly, we should mention that we have made every effort to trace and acquire relevant copyrights in the various elements that make up this book. If anyone has any further information that they could provide in this regard, however, we would be very grateful to receive it.

INTRODUCTION

Although he was not created with posterity in mind, Hank Janson has become something of a cultural signifier, remembered along with ration books and powdered eggs as part of British life in the austere years following the end of World War II. His books were bestsellers, 100,000 copies of each new Hank Janson novel rolling off the presses every six to eight weeks to be sold the length and breadth of the United Kingdom. Physically slim compared to most paperbacks nowadays, and with beautifully painted covers by (bar a couple of exceptions) Reginald (Heade) Webb, the Janson novels promised a world of excitement and sex in a country still struggling to come to terms with the terrible cost of the war, not just in lives lost but in the need to rebuild itself as a nation and as a world power.

It is unlikely that Hank Janson would have become famous (or, rather, infamous) at any other time. Paper supplies from Europe and Africa, cut off during the war, had led to a shortage of reading material in the days before television took the place of literature as the prime source of entertainment. Enterprising publishers had sprung up to take advantage, printing on whatever they could find; as paper became more plentiful, the more successful of these new publishers filled the niche left by import restrictions imposed to help pay off the debts arising from the Lend-Lease agreement with America. These restrictions made importing American books financially unsound, and the cheap paperback publishers found an audience for *faux* American crime novels in the style of Peter Cheyney and James Hadley Chase. For a few years the market for these violent, sexually charged novels seemed insatiable, until a series of court cases were instigated by the Home Office to shut down the publishers.

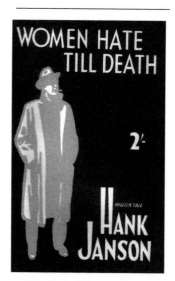

The first edition of *Women Hate Till Death* in 1951 appeared minus a Reginald Heade cover painting, in an attempt by the publishers to avoid further obscenity prosecutions.

8

Although he was billed as the "Best of Tough Gangster Authors", and briefly as "Britain's Best Selling American Author", Hank Janson was home grown, the creation of Stephen Daniel Frances, born in South London in 1917. Frances had begun writing as a way of expressing his political views and highlighting the poor working conditions he saw around him in the 1930s. During the war he was a conscientious objector, self-publishing a duplicated political magazine called *Free Expression* and living in a converted bus, bought cheaply at a wrecker's yard, on a plot of land near the Thames at Shepperton. O ne of his neighbours for a while was Harry Whitby, holidaying with his wife in a caravan; he and Frances struck up a friendship and Whitby, a doctor with a private income and a fascination for gambling, offered to finance a small publishing venture. Pendulum

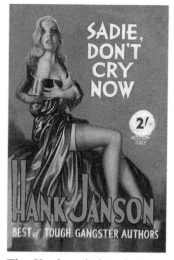

The Heade painting that was used on an ultra-rare reissue of the later Series Three book *Sadie, Don't Cry Now* is believed to have been the one originally intended to appear on the first edition of *Women Hate Till Death.*

Publications was launched in 1944, with Frances as managing director.

After struggling with paper and distribution for a couple of years, Harry Whitby decided to move on, and Pendulum was sold; it's new owners almost immediately went bankrupt, leaving Frances unpaid for his shares but with many contacts in the publishing business. O n a limited budget, and knowing that he would need to turn over any publication quickly to make a profit, Frances pounded out a western in a few weeks and printed up 10,000 copies, selling the whole print run to distributor Julius Reiter of Gaywood Press at a knock-down discount. Reiter suggested that rather than publishing the follow-up western he was working on, Frances should make his next book a crime novel.

Frances had earlier produced three short crime stories to capitalize on some paper that had come his way during his Pendulum days. Reviving their lead character - Hank Janson - he began churning out novel after novel, selling the whole print run to Reiter and ploughing the money back into his business, buying paper and cover artwork, paying for reprints of earlier novels and branching out to launch other lines for other publishers who were becoming aware that there was more to the writing of this new author than the usual hack-work they were printing.

9

Not that the early Janson novels were anything more than reasonably good pulp adventures. The America that Janson travelled through was not the world of Big Jim Colosimo, Johnny Torrio, Alphonse "Scarface" Capone and other prohibition gangsters, but a post-war America drawn mostly from holiday guides; Frances sketched in a background seeded with a few facts about the location and then wrote thrillers that, more often than not, could have been set anywhere.

In his favour, it must be said that Frances favoured stories that avoided the cliches of his British contemporaries. He soon found the character's metier when Hank became a reporter on the *Chicago Chronicle* and Frances was able to begin building a cast of colleagues and social settings for his central character. If you've read Janson in the past, you'll be aware that the novels were published in series of twelve; these significant changes were made with the (lucky) thirteenth novel to carry the Hank Janson byline, *Sister, Don't Hate Me*.

There were more significant changes as the second series came to an end: the opening of the third series was a risky experiment as, for five consecutive novels, Janson, the character, made no appearance at all. During 1949 and 1950, Frances had also produced a steady stream of straightforward gangster thrillers for other publishers under various bylines to finance higher print runs of Janson's adventures; by late 1950 he was able to stop writing these and concentrate on his own publishing venture. Toward the tail end of the second series of Janson novels, he published *No Flowers For The Dead* (as by Max Clinten) in the hope that lightning would strike twice and he could launch a new series of novels that would match the popularity of Janson, but it was not to be. Instead, Frances used the selling power of the Janson byline for his non-Janson novels; a significant move in that it showed that Frances had learned that he could not shoehorn Hank into every novel if Hank was to develop as a consistent character (a problem that had led to some patchy stories in the first two series).

The cover design was slightly amended for this '8th Edition' reissue, to achieve consistency with a range of Janson reissues that appeared in the mid-1950s.

Women Hate Till Death was the second novel in the third series to feature Janson as a reporter on the *Chronicle* and the first to capitalize on the earlier experiment, removing Hank from a considerable portion of the book as he listens to the story of Doris and Marion Langham, two cousins who undergo a horrific ordeal in a Nazi women's camp in Poland. Although war had been an important facet of his first novel, *One Man In His Time*, and World War II specifically would be the setting for two later Janson novels, *Revolt* and *Invasion*, this was the first time that Frances had dealt fully with its atrocities. Although the story of the women's camp is interwoven with the story of Janson's investigation of a murder, the book was breaking new ground, written in 1951 when very few novels were so directly concerned

The edited reissue published by Alexander Moring Ltd in 1958 appeared under the abbreviated title *Hate*.

with the war, let alone the harrowing trials of women prisoners caught up in the conflict. Certainly few other novels would have had anything like the circulation or the impact of Janson's two-shilling "crime thriller".

The novel is not without its faults, but fifty years on it still retains its chilling atmosphere. Starkly told with flashes of disturbing detail, it shows Frances walking the fine line between telling an unsettling story and presenting something too distressing to be comfortably read. To alleviate some of the tension, he introduced into the narrative a rival reporter - Jenny Finton of the *Echo* - and the book achieves just the right balance between its lighter moments and its graphically told back story; a skill Frances honed swiftly over the course of writing fifty novels in three years.

If this is your first taste of Hank Janson, welcome to the terse, tense world of the "Best of Tough Gangster Authors". *Women Hate Till Death* (here restored to its uncut glory and published for the first time with a previously unused Heade cover) remains a remarkable, disquieting novel that will leave you begging for more.

Steve Holland
Colchester, February 2003

WOMEN HATE TILL DEATH

CHAPTER ONE

There were maybe a coupla hundred folk at that reception and a lotta them were Brass. Army Brass, Navy Brass and Air Force Brass. The large room had been specially garlanded for the occasion, flags of all nations hung from the walls, stiff-shirted waiters glided obsequiously among the guests with well-loaded trays and you could hear every kind of accent from Texas to Washington. It was a very select reception. You didn't hear the Brooklyn or Bowery accent.

I was bored. Maybe this was an event for most of the folk around me. It was a pain in the neck for me. I've attended many such functions, learned from experience their news value is nil and the free drinks a bid to buy publicity for the party throwing the reception.

You could recognise the organisers right off. They were mingling freely, being good fellas, going from group to group saying a few polite words.

The Brass treated the reception like a reunion dinner, greeted each other effusively, wrung each other's hands while their wives criticised one another's tea gowns with glassy smiles.

Of course, they weren't all Brass. There were representatives of engineering companies, motor-tyre manufacturers' representatives, electrical specialists, steel manufacturers from Detroit and guys whose firms made unbreakable glass.

And, of course, there was ... the press!

There were maybe half-a-dozen of our boys around. They included Jenny Finton of the *Echo*. In the same way the Brass split itself into groups and talked shop, so the newshounds formed a group. A group around Jenny.

I'd have been with the group myself except for one thing. Jenny! Not that I have anything against Jenny. She's one of the best, an attractive brunette, loaded with guts and determination and a first-rate newspaper woman. But the previous week Jenny and I were in competition to get a story. I got the story first. It was my job to get the story first. It so happened that just before I phoned my story to the Editor, Jenny Finton was inexplicably locked in the gentleman's powder-room. She had the idea I'd double-crossed her. A certain coolness had developed between us. A coolness that could be better described as murderous anger on her part and a guilty feeling inside me that said I'd over-stepped the mark.

Time heals all wounds. Doubtless, when her wound had healed we should be sipping cider through the same straw once again. But in the meantime it was smart to keep out of her way, not probe the injury. Anyway, she'd already seen me. Her eyes had rested upon me momentarily when I entered. She'd been way across the room and the contempt in her eyes sent cold shudders down my back. I didn't wanna see her close up.

I drained my drink, stopped a passing waiter, helped myself to another glass. There were salted-almonds on the tray. I took a handful, chewed them thoughtfully and slowly, watching everybody talking and laughing and feeling strangely lonely and out of things.

It was looking around that way I noticed the dames, two of them, ages maybe twenty-four or twenty-five. They looked like I felt - out of things. They were sitting on a settee side by side, not talking but looking around like they hoped someone would notice them. Almost without realising it, I was drifting in their direction. Maybe it was on account I wanted company, maybe on account they were nice-looking dames, maybe on account one of them sat with crossed legs, showing a slim leg and a daintily poised halter-shoe.

Without looking at them directly, I drifted alongside their table, put down my glass. A few moments later I picked it up again, made a mistake, nearly picked up their glass. I smiled an apology. The dame with the crossed legs smiled back. She had brown eyes, a slightly up-tilted nose, which gave her a cheeky expression, dimpled cheeks and a tiny dimple in her chin.

The other dame merely stared at me. She was beautiful in a cold kinda way. Large expressive eyes and firm, clear-cut features. She had the kinda beauty you find sculptured on the faces of Greek goddesses. A beauty to be admired and a beauty which endures. But there was no softness about her beauty, no endearing quality which makes a guy feel good. One dazzling smile would have transformed her into a living goddess; but her mouth was too sad, too dignified and set to smile. Her wide expressive eyes reflected the merest trace of hostility.

"Taking a time to get on with it," I said conversationally.

The dame who'd smiled, smiled some more. "Everybody's so interested in themselves they've forgotten what they came for."

"That's the way with the Brass," I commented.

She dimpled a smile, her eyes sparkled. "You're not in the service yourself?"

14

"I stopped playing with tin soldiers the first day I clambered out of my cradle without help."

Her cheeks dimpled more. "You're not likely to know my brother then?"

"I might do," I said cautiously. It was easy to figure her brother's name would be her name, unless she was married. There weren't any rings on her fingers that I could see.

"Major John Langham," she told me. "Transport Section."

"No," I told her. "I don't know him."

She smiled ruefully. "I suppose it's typical of the military. Invites me to this reception and at the last minute he's called away to Washington." She chuckled. "I can't imagine how he thinks I can make him a report on this. I know simply nothing about it."

"Don't worry," I said reassuringly. "Collect the clippings from the newspapers. They'll give all you want and more."

She smiled, crossed her legs, toyed with her empty glass meaningfully.

"Shall I ... ?"

"If you'd be so kind," she smiled prettily.

I took her empty glass, looked at her companion enquiringly. The wide eyes looked at me emotionlessly. She shook her head ever so slightly as though I was worthy of only the minimum effort of attention demanded by etiquette.

I found a waiter at the far end of the room, obtained two more filled glasses, and when I got back there was more room on the divan, almost as though they'd deliberately moved along. I accepted the hint, politely murmured a request and sat beside Dimples.

"You connected with the car industry?" she asked.

"Reporter," I sighed. "We get our nose in on everything. The interesting stuff and the dull."

"You don't find this interesting?"

I looked at her; laughing eyes stared into mine. "I didn't; not until a few moments ago." I said it quietly so her companion wouldn't hear.

She gave a husky chuckle of merriment, turned away to sip at her drink and cover up her embarrassment. She couldn't hide the soft flush that coloured her cheeks, made her eyes seem to sparkle even more brightly.

I leaned back in the seat, crossed my legs, toyed with my glass, rolling the long thin stem between forefinger and thumb. "My name's Hank," I told her. "Hank Janson."

"I suppose that means I should introduce myself."

"That'd be real sociable."

"My name's Doris," she said. "Doris Langham."

15

"Pleased to meetcha, Doris. What about your friend? Can't she talk?"

Doris's face hardened slightly, as did the tone in her voice. She didn't like me referring to her friend that way. She said almost severely, "Marion is a very good friend of mine. She happens to be my cousin. Marion Langham, meet Hank Janson."

I sat up, stretched my arm across in front of Doris. The wide eyes stared at me, her head inclined in reluctant acknowledgement and her fingers slipped in and out of mine, barely touching them. I noticed her fingers were cold, like ice.

I withdrew my arm and Doris sucked in her breasts quickly so my arm just missed brushing against her bodice. "Marion's got a headache," she said swiftly. "She's not feeling too well."

"Gee, that's too bad," I drawled. "Maybe I can ..."

Things were happening at last. The organisers were gathered in a group and the chairman of the car manufacturing company throwing this reception stood on a chair, announced loudly that the demonstration would take place outside in ten minutes and would everybody take their seats at their leisure.

It was the most natural thing in the world to stick with the two girls, drift outside with them. When you're with two dames, the most interesting place is in the middle. I inserted myself between them, as we strolled towards the exit. Marion, just as discreetly, stooped suddenly to adjust her shoe, caught up with us, went the other side, kept Doris between us as a buffer. I was getting the certain feeling Marion was allergic to men, feeling happier the further she was from them.

It was a good day for the demonstration with only a little wind and a bright sun. We'd had a chance to inspect the car before the drinks were served. It was a nice job, streamlined and mechanically sound. To make it, however, had cost fifty times as much as any other car the same size. Everybody understood why. It was experimental. The first atomic car ever made.

The steward provided everyone with time-sheets and pencils. A large board gave details of the length of each run. An enormous clock with a second hand was placed where everyone could see it.

The car drove up and down a coupla times, warming up and demonstrating its artistic lines. Then the chequered flag waved and the car took the track heading to our left, speeding rapidly and loudly until it was out of sight. I strained my eyes and could just see the distant red post which marked the beginning of the measured two-mile course.

We couldn't see the car when it turned and hurtled back, gathering momentum so it should reach the starting post at maximum speed. But we could hear it. As deafening as a fleet of tanks. It passed the starting post like a tracer bullet, tore down the track towards us with a sound like a thousand canvas sails being ripped in two.

It zipped past us, blurred red movement rapidly diminishing towards the finishing post. It disappeared beyond our vision, the engine roars still audible as the car was turned for its return run.

The model made a lotta noise and looked plenty speedy. But the actual timed records were nothing exceptional. A hundred and ten miles an hour. On straight, wide American roads, that speed was used plenty by high-powered passenger cars.

The car roared back along the track a second time. It notched a coupla extra miles per hour to its speed. It still wasn't impressive. But then, speed wasn't the real test for this car. The real test was adaptability. If this experimental car should prove itself, atomic-powered cars would become the cars of the future, the running costs almost negligible and the consequent saving of gasoline ensuring that the apparently inexhaustible oil-wells of America would never run dry.

On the third run the car began to lose speed rapidly almost as soon as it passed the starting post. The car swerved crazily as the driver frantically applied his brakes. The explosive throbbing that filled the air cut off abruptly as the driver killed the engine, and in the hushed silence that followed, you could hear tyres screeching on the gravel and the low whine as brake drums growled a protest against the straining pressure.

He managed to stop the car, travelling the last twenty yards broadside like a crab. If he had planned it, the car couldn't have stopped in a better position. It was set dead square in front of the audience. And as the driver frantically scrambled from his seat we could all see the trouble. The engine was built in the rear of the car. It was a big engine and the car had a long tail. Throughout those two short test runs, particles of atoms had been bombarding each other at tremendous velocities. There'd been a leakage somewhere. The bombardment hadn't confined itself to the interior of the engine.

I wasn't surprised the driver was in a hurry to leave his seat. The whole of the tail of the car glowed a bright cherry red, the paint smoking as it burned on the red hot metal. Even as the driver jumped clear of the car, the upholstered back of his driving seat burst into flames.

Well, it was a nice try. Few things are perfect the first time. They're rarely perfect even the hundredth time. The pity was they'd given so much publicity to this demonstration before finding out it was a good way to fry the driver.

There was a lotta excitement, white-overalled officials running out on the track, Red Cross men inspecting the driver's hands, and the driver gingerly massaging the seat of his pants. The smiles on the faces of the organisers had slipped, but they steered everybody back to the reception hall, said nobody was to worry, that these things often happen.

The two dames' reactions were a startling contrast. Throughout the test, Doris had been keyed up, eyes sparkling excitedly, hands clenched tightly as the car roared past her, and then straining forward eagerly to watch it out of her sight.

Marion sat in her seat stonily, impenetrable, watching with wide, lack-lustre eyes not even willing to move her head the tiniest bit in order to see a little better.

"Gee, I was scared," confessed Doris breathlessly. She rested her fingers on her breast as though to still the pounding of her heart. "I really thought he was going to turn over. All that loose gravel flying around, too. The people down there musta got covered."

"It's unlucky for everyone," I said. "They've probably made that run a hundred times without this trouble. Then on the very day they demonstrate, an unexpected snag crops up." I shrugged. "I suppose that's what makes life go on, setbacks continually occurring and folks trying to set them right."

"Was he really burnt, do you think?"

I grinned. "Not much. He quit the car too quick." I turned to Marion. "How did it strike you?"

She half-turned her head, moved her eyes so I should know she was speaking to me. "I can't really say," she said coldly. "I know nothing about these things."

There was a long, cold, awkward pause. I took a deep breath, said masterfully, "Let's go get a drink."

That seemed to be everybody's idea. The waiters glided around with trays that were emptied as soon as they were loaded. I caught a waiter fresh off the mark, selected three glasses and carefully carried them to the table where the two dames were sitting. I pulled out a pack of cigarettes, offered them. While I did so I gave the dames the once-over. Marion was dressed neatly in black, a neatly tailored suit. The jacket flared out stiffly from her hips, and the skirt was tight and knee-length. The jacket was buttoned discreetly, and her white silk blouse had a frilly front that looked like a cravat.

Marion's attire was like her, discrete, quiet and self-assured.

Doris also wore clothes that were like her. A knee-length black frock, pleated skirt with a silver-worked design on her bodice. She wore two gold bracelets around her right wrist, a fine chain around her right ankle and a fur cape.

18

Those two girls were as different as chalk and cheese. But I sensed there was an intimate bond between them, an understanding which went deeper than mere friendship.

I held a match for Doris and as she bent forward to draw on her cigarette, her eyes raised towards mine. I knew her vanity was tickled by my interest in her. And as though to encourage my interest, once again she crossed her legs, the skirt this time riding up to just above her knee.

"Your home town Chicago?" I asked conversationally.

She flashed a smile, opened her mouth to reply. But the organisers had got busy again, one of them standing on a chair to make an announcement. The buzz of voices died away, everybody craned their necks to hear what he had to say.

He smiled around. "I'm sorry about the breakdown in the plans," he said bluntly. "In just a minute we'll have some specially drawn plans here. I want to show you exactly the difficulties we're up against."

Doris re-crossed her legs. Her foot caught the fragile table, rocked it so her handbag, placed on the edge, toppled, hit the floor and burst open. Little bottles and other toilet accessories rolled on the floor.

The organiser and the guests turned to stare at her. She blushed, stooped down with me, shovelled the contents hastily back into the handbag, including a vanity case which dribbled white powder over the floor and into the bag. "Excuse me," she muttered, red-faced, and hurried away with her bag towards the powder-room.

The organiser cleared his throat, the guests looked back to him and he continued with an involved, verbal description of why the demonstration car had become overheated.

While he was talking, two porters carried in an easel and blackboard, erected it behind him. The organiser transferred himself from the chair to the front of the blackboard, drew knowledgeable sweeping symbols with the chalk, talked glibly about isotopes, nuclear fissions and electronic bombardments.

"To give you an even clearer idea ..."

He broke off, stood on tip-toe. "Have you got that chart yet?" he called.

There was a stir. Someone bearing a large roll of canvas like a large-scale map was pushing through the audience toward the organiser. Folk made way for him, the organiser stood back as the man adjusted the chart on the blackboard, allowed it to unroll its full length. He stood back and I got my first real look at him, a chubby, dark-haired guy, medium height with a small dark moustache. He was maybe about forty. The organiser nodded his head in thanks, picked up a wooden pointer and started to continue his lecture.

The pointer froze in mid-air, his mouth gaped, soundlessly opened to speak, and all the heads craned around in my direction. My own head jerked around too. Because Marion had risen to her feet, was staring with wide, black eyes towards the organiser. Her mouth was forced wide, jawbone prominently showing through flesh as she let loose a series of nerve-wracking shrieks.

Those screams almost weren't human. It was as though she'd suddenly received spasms of unbearable and unbelievable agony. It was so unexpected, so completely without reason that like everyone else I gaped in astonishment. Then from the corner of my eye I caught a glimpse of Doris, eyes and face registering desperate anxiety as she shouldered through the audience, fighting towards us.

It was lucky I was there, because Doris wouldn't have been in time. One more gasping scream jerked itself from Marion's lips. Then her head went back, her eyes closed and her knees sagged.

I reached her just in time, got my hands beneath her armpits as she went down.

Doris was with me a moment later. "Get her out of here," she urged frantically. "Get her out of this place."

The heads craned, the audience moved in on us. Somewhere a table went over and there was the splintering of broken glasses. An Army officer wearing enough brass to make a cannon, stabbed his finger towards me, said in commanding tones: "Give her brandy. That's what she wants. Give her brandy."

I kept my arm around her shoulder, slipped my other arm below the back of her knees and lifted. She was amazingly light, almost weightless.

"That's right," panted Doris. "Get her out of here." And she led the way, making urgent motions with her hands so the folk who pressed close to see reluctantly widened to make a passage for us.

Outside the reception room, Red Cross men offered their assistance. Doris brushed them away, whispered to me urgently: "I've got to get her home."

I was still carrying Marion in my arms. "Listen," I protested. "Those guys know what they're up to. It's their business. Let them take a look at her."

"I've gotta get her home," she said between her teeth. "I've gotta get her away from here." She almost stamped her foot at the obstinacy on my face. "Don't be awkward," she pleaded. "Help me when I ask you."

I looked down at Marion. She was out cold, lying limp in my arms like there wasn't a bone in her body. Her face was white, her lips bloodless and a little pucker of worry or pain crossing her forehead.

"Please," pleaded Doris. "Please help me."

"Okay," I said gruffly. "Lead on."

The Red Cross guys watched reluctantly as we walked towards the exit. Doris spun around, stared at me hopelessly. "I've gotta have a taxi," she said. "Ask somebody to get me a taxi."

"Straight ahead, lady," I said. "Straight through that door. We'll use my car."

CHAPTER TWO

Marion was still out cold when we got to the apartment block. I parked out front. Doris, her face full of worry, led the way up the broad steps into the entrance hall.

The elevator hop stared with round eyes as I carried Marion past him into the lift. Her legs hung limply and one shoe fell from her dainty foot. Doris bent, picked it up.

The elevator hop got the lift moving. Then he turned and stared at Marion's white face. "She ain't a gonna, is she, mister?" he asked in a hushed voice.

"Sure," I said. "I just cut her throat. Now we're gonna hide the body."

His eyes rolled to mine, wide and startled.

"Aw, don't tell him that," snapped Doris. "He's a crazy kid. He'll believe anything." She turned to him, spoke loudly and deliberately, like her words were nails she was driving into a solid piece of wood. "This is Miss Langham. You know her, don't you? She's not dead. You can see that, can't you? She's still breathing. She's fainted. D'you understand that? She's not well. She's fainted. Do you understand?"

His eyes rolled from me to Marion, from Marion to Doris. His head nodded slowly, unbelievingly. The lift had eased to a standstill before Doris finished talking. He didn't seem to have noticed it.

"You figure we oughta get this place furnished if we're gonna stop here all night?" I asked him.

He stared at me blankly. "Furnished?"

Doris sighed loudly. "He means open up," she said clearly. "Open the lift gates. We're at the third floor."

He jumped with startled understanding, fumbled nervously and too hastily at the gates, trapping his boot in the sliding door.

Doris led the way along the corridor to her apartment. I was still carrying Marion in my arms like she was a baby. I followed her, and the elevator hop stared after us with round, worried eyes. I could sense his stupid, dimly understanding gaze concentrated between my shoulders. I stopped, turned slowly, stared at him. He stared back. His mouth hung open. I screwed my face into an ugly, threatening menace, growled deep down in my chest.

He disappeared like a flash, there one moment, gone the next like the flame of a candle that's been blown out. He shut the lift door so quickly, it merely shimmered with movement. As the sound of the slammed gate died away, I could still hear him frantically cranking the controls, crazy to get moving.

He sure was a dumb kid. He'd forgotten to close the outer gate. But that elevator hop could move when he wanted. When he opened the lift gate, closed the outer gate and shut the inner gate again, the speed he did it defied imagination. Just a swift flicker of arms, the sliding movement of doors and the sound as they crashed into place.

"Hey," said Doris. "You leaving or coming?"

I turned around. She was holding open the door of an apartment. I pushed past her.

"Straight through," she said. "Go through the lounge, the bedroom on the right."

I carried Marion through into an exquisitely feminine bedroom with tables, windows, alcoves and beds draped with daintily flounced organdie tied with big bows.

I deposited Marion on the bed while Doris fluttered around like an anxious hen.

"Help me take her coat off," she instructed.

It was amusing. Marion was still out cold. I propped her up, Doris eased the coat off her shoulders.

"It's not right," I said anxiously. "If it was just a faint she should have come around before this."

"She's getting me worried too," confessed Doris. "Just make her comfortable, will you?"

I propped pillows beneath her head, eased off her other shoe and opened the top two buttons of her blouse. Meanwhile, Doris was telephoning for a doctor, insisting he came at once.

I rested my fingers on Marion's forehead. It was as cold as ice. So was her hand when I took it to feel her pulse. There wasn't anything wrong with her pulse, beating strong and regular. But holding her wrist that way, I noticed the blue marks etched indelibly on her arm. I stared at them, wondered gently, replaced her arm at her side and said nothing. This wasn't the time to ask questions.

Doris said breathlessly, "The doctor will be here shortly. I think I should get her to bed, so if you'll ..."

"Sure," I said. I looked at Marion and then at Doris. I know how difficult it is to handle someone unconscious. "Don't take this the wrong way," I said. "But if I can help..."

She flashed me a dazzling smile of thanks. "I'll manage," she said. "I'll just slip off her outer things."

I drifted off into the lounge, half-closing the door behind me. She called through it. "Help yourself to a drink, will you? Pour a brandy too. Maybe Marion should have some."

I poured the brandy first, knocked on the half-open door. Doris's arm came around, took the glass. I went back to the cabinet, poured myself Scotch. It was early evening now, time I phoned in my report. I cradled the receiver, dialled the office and dictated a brief story on the failure of the demonstration.

When I hung up, Doris called softly. "Come in, will you, Hank? See what you think of her."

She was conscious now, tucked up in bed with the coverlet around her neck and her face almost as white as the pillows supporting her head. The brandy had served some purpose. Her eyes were open now. But I preferred them shut to the way they were vacantly staring into space. It was like her eyes were frozen, hard black pools staring expressionlessly into nowhere. It was as though she was living but dead, only the gentle rise and fall of the coverlet showing she still breathed.

I asked softly: "Does she know you?"

Doris shook her head. Her eyes were worried. "Marion," she pleaded. "Say something."

The black eyes stared unmovingly, her brain untouched by sight, sound or feeling.

"She ever been like this before?" I asked anxiously.

Doris nodded her head slowly. "Once before," she said slowly, and shuddered. "Once before she was like this."

"What is it?"

"Shock," she said. "The human brain can stand so much then, finish!"

I gulped. "Is she in trouble of some kind?"

She shook her head sadly. "No trouble at all, except for memories."

"How long does she go being this way?"

Her eyes hardened, became strangely grim and bitter. "The last time it lasted six months."

I stared at her incredulously. "You mean, lying still like this? Not knowing anybody or able to look after herself?"

Doris said dully. "It was bad for the first two months. After that she dressed herself, moved around, even fed herself. But her mind was dead like it is now, eyes looking into nowhere and not hearing or seeing anybody."

"She doesn't need a doctor," I said meaningfully. "She wants a specialist."

She sighed. "You wouldn't understand," she said. "You couldn't."

I sensed something strange behind her words, something dark and hidden. There was that mark too on Marion's arm. There were a dozen questions quivering on my tongue that Doris's tense, worried face prevented me from asking, as did the sudden ringing of the door bell.

24

"That'll be the doctor," said Doris.

"I'll get it."

I opened up for him, a slick young fella with an urgent, earnest air. "Where is she?" he asked.

I nodded.

He strode across the room, unlatching his little leather bag as he walked.

I draped myself in the doorway, watched him as he went to work. He held her pulse with one hand, fumbled his stethoscope from his bag with the other. He pulled her slip to one side, listened to her heart-beat while he rolled back her eyelid, inspected her eyes. Then he fumbled in the bag, came up with a pencil torch, shone it into Marion's eyes, squinted so close up to her that his chin was almost resting on hers.

He sat up straight on the side of the bed, whistled to himself noiselessly as he stared thoughtfully at his stethoscope, then said to Doris: "I'd like to make a thorough examination. Would you be good enough ...?"

"Of course," said Doris. She began to pull down the coverlet.

I drifted out, shut the door behind me. I helped myself to more Scotch, paced the room. It was maybe twenty minutes later before the door opened and they both came out. Twenty minutes was a long time for a young doctor in a hurry. He didn't seem in a hurry any longer. His brow was furrowed thoughtfully. He waited until Doris closed the door and clasped her hands, waiting patiently for his decision, then said: "Has she recently been submitted to some severe excitement? Something that would upset her fundamentally, completely demoralising her?"

Doris fluttered her hands nervously. Her eyes flicked to me, then back to the doctor. "Why no," she said. "It was quite unexpected. She went down quite suddenly."

"Hm," said the doctor non-commitally, and rubbed his chin thoughtfully. "It's shock," he said. "A severe case of shock. There's nothing physically wrong to worry about. It's her mind retreating into itself. Trying to escape from something she finds unbearable."

Doris's eyes were moist with tears. "How long ... I mean, is she ..."

"She may snap out of it quickly," he said. His face became serious. "On the other hand, it's possible she'll take a turn for the worse." He shrugged his shoulders. "One can never tell."

"Is there anything I can do for her?"

"Watch her," he said. "Watch her day and night. Get her to eat and drink if you can. But you've got to watch her until she snaps out of it or until she ..." he broke off, licked his lips nervously.

"Until what?" I interrupted rudely.

He inspected his nails gravely. "She may crack," he said quietly.

25

"Meaning what?"

His eyes switched to mine, calculated what he should tell me. "She may crack completely," he said quietly. "Raving, injuring herself and other people. May have to be held down."

Doris caught her breath with a sharp sob. A tear crawled down across her cheek.

He wouldn't look at her. "I'll be around in the morning," he said gruffly.

I saw him to the door, closed it behind him and went back to Doris. She was shredding her handkerchief. "Isn't it terrible, Hank?" she wailed. "Isn't it terrible. After all she's gone through."

"It's gonna be all right," I said comfortingly. "She'll snap out of it any time now."

"I hope so," she said. "I hope so."

I opened the bedroom door, looked at Marion. She was lying there, head propped on the pillows and staring straight at me. At least, it looked that way until I moved. Then her eyes were staring past me. There was something horrible about the blankness of her eyes. I heard an echo of the doctor's words. *She may crack. If she does, she may do injury to herself and others with her.*

I turned back to Doris. "Hey," I said with mock cheerfulness. "How about rustling up some grub? I'm peckish."

"If you want," she said half-heartedly.

"That's no way to treat a guest," I said. "If I'm gonna sit up half the night with you, I wanna do it on a full stomach."

She stared at me. "Sit up half the night?"

"I'm not leaving you here alone," I said firmly. "Not tonight anyway. You may ... need me."

She understood. The echo of the doctor's words was lingering in her ears too. She just said quietly: "Thank you. I do appreciate it." But her eyes expressed her thanks profusely.

"Come on, snap it up," I growled. "Brew some coffee and make it hot. And careful with the can-opener."

She worked up a smile, blinked the tears from her eyelids. "Coming up," she said, in mock, soda-jerk's tones. "Two hot-dawgs coming up wid two cawfees."

She didn't cook badly at that. Steak, chips and eggs thrown together in an amazingly short space of time. She hardly ate anything herself, pecked at her food, pushed it away barely touched.

Her coffee was good too. We drank it in the lounge, sitting on the settee, which was turned around to face Marion's bedroom. We left the door open, Marion in full view so we could see if any change took place.

"How long ago since she was like this?"

26

She lit a cigarette, and her hand was shaking slightly. "Some years," she replied. She shuddered slightly.

"It's no good worrying," I said. "She'll get over it all right. She's got to."

Her face was strangely drawn. "I thought I should never have to worry again."

I eyed her cautiously. "What does that mean?"

She summoned up a brave smile. "I guess I'm not quite myself, hardly know what I'm saying."

I drew on my cigarette, allowed leaden seconds to seep past. "What nationality is Marion?"

She looked at me quickly, one eyebrow arched in surprise. "American, of course. Good old Middle West. Why?"

"I figured she might be a foreigner."

"Why?" she persisted.

I shrugged. "I noticed her arm ..." With my finger I indicated on my own arm where I'd seen the mark.

Doris's eyes stared into mine for about a year. "I'm an American too," she said at last. The sleeve of her black dress was tight. She had difficulty in pulling it up away from the wrist high enough so I could see the tattooed number on her arm. "You didn't have to be a foreigner to get those," she said bitterly.

"I didn't realise," I said. "I thought that ..."

"It's not usual," she admitted. "But it did happen to some people. It happened to me and Marion."

The way she said it, the bitterness in her voice, the smouldering anger inside her that would never be quenched, changed her into a different person. As she sat there, I could sense the pent-up hate inside her.

"I don't see it," I said. "You're American. I don't see how ..."

"That was the cause of Marion," she said fiercely. "That's why she's this way. That's why ..." She broke off like she was choking back something she couldn't be saying.

"Where did it happen?" I probed gently.

"Czechoslovakia," she said quietly.

"What were you doing there?"

Her lips curled in a bitter smile. "I was on holiday. That's how it happened for me. It was different for Marion. She was living there."

"Living there?"

She nodded. "She'd been living there with her family in Czechoslovakia for four or five years. When Germany invaded Czechoslovakia, Marion's father stayed on. He had a sound job with an American firm and felt it was his duty to remain."

"Weren't restrictions imposed on him?"

27

"A few," she said. "Trifling little restrictions that were unimportant." She chuckled ruefully. "Marion's my cousin. For a long time I'd wanted to visit Europe. For a long time Marion's family had invited me to pay them a visit. It was just my luck, I guess. I accepted their invitation at the wrong time, had been in Czechoslovakia with them only two weeks when America came into the war."

I nodded my head understandingly. "You all became enemy aliens and were interned."

Her eyes were hard when she shook her head. "Nothing so easy as that, brother," she said bitterly. "Nothing so easy as that!"

"D'you wanna talk about it?" I asked.

She looked towards Marion, bit her lip and said softly: "It would help you to understand. You'd know then why it's this way."

CHAPTER THREE

We had time on our hands, sitting there and watching Marion, waiting for the long hours to pass. It was natural we should talk and natural that Doris should tell me what happened in Czechoslovakia. But when folks are talking, their conversation is disjointed, there are interruptions and side-issues.

I'm gonna tell the story Doris told me. But I'm gonna tell it in my own words. I shan't omit anything, or add anything. I'll give the blunt facts as she gave them to me. I'll build a mind picture of those things as she built them in my mind.

Pearl Harbour was bombed after Doris had been with Marion's family a fortnight. The next day the United States declared war on Germany. That was curtains for the few American citizens still remaining in Czechoslovakia. It was internment camp for most and, in some cases, special arrangements were made for them to return home.

Marion's father occupied a responsible position. Immediately following the declaration of war, he was visited by the police, told he was under house-arrest. That included Doris and Marion. Meanwhile, Marion's father made application through official circles for the return of his family to America.

Two or three days later the formalities were nearing completion, official forms and letters had been signed and a reservation made for them on a train going through to Switzerland.

At that point everything went wrong. Maybe it was bad luck, maybe it was deliberate, the German authorities seizing at an opportunity that presented itself.

A British bombing raid had taken place, causing great devastation and loss of life. Public feeling was running very high. To such an extent German police were posted around Marion's home as a protective measure. This fact alone made nonsense of what transpired later. Because not only could the irate Czechs not obtain entrance to Marion's home, but likewise, her family could not get out past the guard.

One of the British planes was shot down. It crashed on the outskirts of the town and two of the crew were killed outright. Six others escaped, four being captured within forty-eight hours and the remaining two successfully evading capture.

Three days after the crash, Marion's family and Doris were charged with assisting and aiding British pilots to escape internment.

The charge was ridiculous. None of them treated it seriously. That is, not until the negotiations for their departure were suddenly broken off, pending their court trial.

In time of peace, no matter how strained that peace might be, it is difficult to imagine a court trial being a travesty of justice, false accusations being given by unreliable witnesses who again and again are caught out in lies by the defending counsel.

But in time of war the moral values change. Incredible as it seems, innocent of the offence with which they had been accused, Doris, Marion, her mother and father, sat in court day after day, listening with mounting apprehension to the volume of circumstantial evidence produced and intoned by the prosecuting counsel. Incredible evidence that on occasions seemed laughable. For example, that Marion's father had applied to the American Embassy for assistance in returning to America, that Doris herself had been seen in the vicinity of a number nine bus while everyone knew the number nine bus route ran to within four miles of the point where the British bomber crashed.

The charge was so ridiculously flimsy it seemed to them incredible it should be taken so seriously in a court of law. They were still in a dream, when they were told to stand, heard their sentence solemnly intoned, learned they were to be imprisoned for life.

Maybe they were lucky to have been so stunned by everything. To be sentenced to imprisonment for life is a terrible thing. To be young and on the threshold of life, as were Marion and Doris at the age of seventeen, and to receive such a sentence must have been hell.

They couldn't believe it. They still couldn't believe it when Marion's mother and father, after just a moment to say their farewells, were taken in one direction, while Marion and Doris were herded to a cell beneath the court and locked in together, awaiting an escort to their place of confinement.

The cell was bare, with just one small bench for them to sit on. They were left without food or water for twenty-four hours. Left to meditate and talk, to realise the hard, bitter truth, to be convinced that their youthful bodies just flowering into womanhood were about to be buried alive, hidden from the sun and the light of human compassion.

Having the heavy door slammed behind them, hearing huge bolts rammed home, was a terrible psychological experience. Twenty-four hours of confinement in that tiny, stone world, cut off from everyone, drained the hope from them, made them desperate, made them feel it would be better to be dead.

Then as the hours passed, hope grew strong inside them again. Of course it was all some gigantic mistake. It would be straightened out. The American authorities would intercede. After a time they would be released. Marion had visited a Czechoslovakian prison with her father. She told Doris about it. It wasn't so bad. The women were locked up two to a cell. The work was hard. But it was not drudgery. There were educational facilities, even an occasional movie show. After the first three months, prisoners were allowed lipstick if they wished, and good conduct prisoners could wear their own clothes.

Yeah, at the end of twenty-four hours they'd talked themselves into a state of resignation, willing to face up to a temporary period of imprisonment with the conviction that Uncle Sam would be striving on their behalf and release would come at any time.

When at last the bolts shot back and the heavy door swung open they were in a resigned, but hopeful frame of mind.

Two cops had come for them. One led the way and the second cop motioned them to follow. He brought up the rear. They were ushered upstairs to an office where three more uniformed cops were waiting together with a plain-clothed detective. Routine questions were asked, their names and other particulars entered on index cards and the detective signed for them. That's just what happened. He signed for possession of their bodies in the way a man would sign for a television set delivered to his doorstep.

Marion complained they'd had nothing to eat or drink for twenty-four hours. The local cops apologised, explained it hadn't been known they would be detained so long. The detective nodded a gruff agreement and the cops made the girls some coffee, handed them large slices of bread and margarine.

They ate ravenously and gratefully; the detective fidgeting all the time, continually looking at his wristwatch, finally gruffly commanding them: "Let's get going. I haven't all day."

A Black Maria was waiting outside. One of the uniformed cops was the driver. The other two cops and the detective climbed into the Black Maria with Marion and Doris, who sat close together. They were kids, just seventeen. They were overawed by everything that was happening, scared by it too. The two cops talked about football, the detective smoked in silence.

"Where are we going?" asked Marion timidly.

The two cops broke off talking, stared at her indignantly and then resumed their conversation. The detective blew smoke through his nostrils, drawled disinterestedly: "You'll find out."

In that lurching, swaying van it was impossible to see anything of the outside world except the square of sky that gleamed through a grating high up in the door. Eventually the van stopped, there were shouting voices, the sound of huge gates being opened and then the van was rolling forward again.

The next time it stopped, the driver hammered on the partition. The cops opened up the door, climbed out and rasped: "Come on you two. Hurry up there."

There was time for a glimpse around the courtyard before they were ushered through a doorway. Marion recognised it at once. It was the very prison she had once visited. She whispered this information to Doris, and the detective growled: "Stop talking. No talking allowed."

They were led along a stone corridor that echoed their footsteps from end to end. The detective stopped outside the door of a cell, swung it open. He jerked his head at them. "In here," he growled. "Wait."

It was bare, except for a wooden bench. When the door clanged shut behind them, only a little light filtered into the cell from a grating far above their heads. The walls were whitewashed brickwork and the floor was stone.

Doris shuddered. "It's dreadful," she said.

Marion tried to cheer her. "Just a little wait," she said. "Then we go to reception. They make a record of all particulars, issue us with a uniform and allocate us a cell. We'll probably share a cell together. And the cells are quite comfortable, good mattresses and warm blankets. You can have all kinds of things in your cell too, books, flowers, pictures, almost anything you want."

"I'm scared," admitted Doris frankly.

"Don't worry," said Marion confidently. "Dad will know what to do. He'll fix everything. Just leave it to him."

Two hours passed. The wooden bench was small and hard, not long enough for two of them to sit side by side. They got up to leave when the bolt slammed back, but the warder thrust two steaming bowls of soup at them, together with two hunks of brown, almost black bread.

It wasn't the type of food they were accustomed to. But they were hungry. They finished the soup, soaked their dry bread in it, savoured it to the last morsel and then wished there were more.

Time passed slowly. So slowly it seemed the whole day had gone, before the door once again opened and a harsh voice directed them outside into the corridor.

It was the same detective, but two different cops. They herded the girls along corridors, up steep stone steps. Twice they passed uniformed wardresses and once they filed across a gallery, where below them grey-clad figures were working amidst the steam of large laundry presses.

Even to Doris, who had never visited a prison in her life, this reception seemed strange. It was almost as though they were being ushered through the prison surreptitiously. That impression became stronger when the detective warned them they were about to meet the Governor of the prison and they passed through what was obviously a back door to his office.

It was a large office with massive furniture. The Governor, a tired-eyed man with white hair, stared at them from across his desk, briefly scrutinizing them before he switched his glance to the fireplace. Draped elegantly against the mantelpiece was a young SS officer. He lounged there, youthful, arrogant and acutely conscious of the power vested in him.

The Governor cleared his throat, looked at the two girls. "Come forward," he said almost kindly. "Come over here." He beckoned them to stand just in front of his desk.

Keeping close to each other as though the contact of their shoulders gave them extra strength, the two girls edged forward. The detective followed right behind them. The two cops, obeying a gesture of the Governor, went out, closed the door behind them.

Marion, having lived in Czechoslovakia many years, understood the language. Doris understood but a few words. But Doris had learned German in America and was able to understand the SS officer when he asked the Governor in hard, curt tones: "These are the Langham girls?"

The Governor nodded wearily. He put one hand to his forehead as though he wanted to rest his head.

The SS officer detached himself from the fireplace and with an insolent, self-conscious bearing, lounged around back of the Governor and stood with his thumbs looped in his belt, staring at the girls so long, they dropped their eyes in embarrassment. He was a young guy. But he wasn't looking at them the way a young guy looks at dames. There was a savage, sadistic glint in his eyes which was terrifying.

"Well, what are we waiting for?" he drawled in German.

The Governor said tiredly to the detective: "Have you got the records?"

"I prefer that you speak in German," snapped the SS officer.

The Governor sighed, repeated his question in German. The detective took the record cards from his inner pocket, held them towards the Governor. The SS officer snatched them impatiently, scrutinised them himself. He snarled at the detective. "These records are those which show these two have been brought to this prison."

The detective nodded. "Yes, sir".

"And there are no other records whatsoever?"

"No other records," the detective assured him.

Slowly and deliberately the SS officer ripped the cards across and across. He dropped the fragments on the desk in front of the Governor. "There is the answer to your problem," he said with a sneer in his voice. "That is *all* that is necessary."

The Governor sighed. He looked from the torn record cards to the girls and then back to the torn cards. "It shall be as you say," he said wearily. He motioned with his hand, and the detective took the girls by the arm. "Come on," he grunted. "That's all."

They were bewildered by it all. They were more bewildered when they were taken back to the cell with the hard bench. They asked questions but the detective ignored them. He thrust them into the cell almost roughly, snarled at them to be quiet, slammed home the door.

"Well, what did you make of that?" asked Marion indignantly. "Not even been to reception yet. How much longer are they going to keep us hanging around?"

Doris said slowly: "I don't like it. There's something strange about it. That SS officer. It means trouble of some kind."

"You're being imaginative," said Marion. "SS men are everywhere. It's part of the system. You ought to know that by now."

"Just the same," said Doris. "I don't like it."

Light faded from the cell and darkness invaded them. Not long later, two bowls of soup were thrust through the door at them with hunks of bread. They had to eat in darkness, and now the sun had gone down it was cold. They were weary too. They took it in turns to lie cramped on the bench trying to sleep, while the other paced the concrete floor, or wearily sank down on the cold stone, braving the cold for the relief of a few moments' relaxation of aching muscles.

The hours dragged by. The cold of the stone entered their bones so their bones ached and they shivered and huddled together for warmth.

Then as the first grey glimmer of dawn came creeping into their cell they heard the crisp rap of jack-boots in the corridor outside. They were ready to leave. Anything was better than this agony, numbed blue and cramped with the cold. When the bolts shot back and the door swung open, they were almost eager to get away from that cell.

It wasn't prison warders. They were SS men, brightly gleaming knee-boots and Sam Browns contrasting to the black of their uniforms. Instinctively Doris shrank back. One of them roughly grabbed her wrists, jerked her forward into the passage. Another grabbed her by the shoulders, propelled her along the corridor to the open door where other SS men stood waiting.

Jack-boots rang out on the stone floor behind them, strong hands grasped their shoulders and arms, propelled them out into the dull grey of early morning. Marion was roughly bundled into the first car, thrust in the back seat while storm-troopers crowded in beside her. She turned her head, desperately scared, saw Doris being bundled into the car behind. That was all she had time to see, because fingers locked in her hair, pulled her head around. "Don't stare around," snarled a voice in German. The owner of it was a slim young boy not much older than herself. He was handsome in a Nordic fashion, fair hair, wide blue eyes and finely-cut features. But there was an inhumanness about him which made her shudder at his touch.

The car jerked into movement. She heard the car behind revving its engine and felt a surge of relief, knowing Doris would not be far away. "Please," she pleaded. "Where are you taking me?"

Nobody answered her. The young faces around her were solemn, like their owners were performing some tremendously important task of the State. One of them said in clear-cut, precise words: "You will please not talk or attempt to engage us in conversation."

"But I only wanted to ..."

The young storm-trooper who had spoken, leaned forward, slapped his fingers hard across her cheek. "You will do as you are instructed," he said coldly.

Marion slumped back in the seat, her eyes moist, and her ears ringing from that stinging blow. The car roared on through the city, through the early-morning streets, where only an occasional early riser glanced around quickly at the sound of the engine, only to look away guiltily as though not wanting to see that which was forbidden.

The car tore along like lost time was to be made up, blasting its hooter imperiously, lurching around street corners. She was crushed between the SS men, who sat stiff, erect and silent around her. She was scared. Suddenly the prison seemed warm and friendly; even that bare stone cell would be a sanctuary from this. And now her stomach turned over with a sudden, agonised fear. The silence of these men in the grey light of dawn, the mad rush through the streets, those slick, shining uniforms and the rifles they carried, convinced her these were her last moments on Earth. This explained everything. Their torn record cards, their segregation at the prison and this early morning, reckless drive through the silent city. She was going to be executed. She realised it with the sharp shock of a physical blow. And fear was wild inside her, possessed her so completely, that when she realised her underclothing was damp and moisture trickled down her legs, she was not ashamed that the silent men around her should know what had happened.

The wild drive continued, the car roaring out into the suburbs. She wondered if she would be blindfolded. She closed her eyes and muttered silent prayers.

The car lurched to a standstill with a loud squealing of brakes. She quivered, moaned piteously, resisted tearfully as they dragged her from the car. Her wild, searching, apprehensive eyes saw many things. The line of dirty railway wagons at the top of the embankment, the car bearing Doris pulling up behind. The contemptuous curl of the lips of the young SS man when he saw the damp patch on the back of her skirt, and the armed guards who paced the railway line beside the wagons.

It was a wild, mixed-up dream. They were going to shoot her, were dragging, forcing her up the embankment towards the stationary train. Doris was behind her. Marion sensed that she too was resisting, struggling futilely. At the top of the embankment she was held firmly. Harsh voices shouted instructions and commands, jack-boots ground gravel underfoot and guards were unslinging their rifles, standing in a semi-circle, pointing their guns at one of the wagons.

She understood none of it, suffered only mind-consuming fear that made her tremble violently, moan piteously, sag weakly in their steely grip and feel afresh the moisture trickling down her legs.

Vaguely she realised it would be just a few moments now. She would be propped against the railway wagon, the pointing rifles pouring hot, burning lead into her young body.

Strange things were happening. Uniformed men were unpadlocking the wagon. The armed guards moved in, formed a smaller semi-circle, pointed their rifles threateningly. The door of the wagon was opened, human faces pressed forward out of the darkness of the wagon only to cower back as the rifles menaced. They were gaunt, grey faces, emaciated, hardly human. Before she could take it in, she was being roughly dragged towards the open doorway. Her feet were lifted, strong hands propelled her so forcibly her skirt was rucked up and her bare buttocks scraped painfully across rough wooden flooring. High-heeled shoes gouged painfully in the small of her back as Doris was thrust in after her, thrust with such force she rolled on top of Marion. As they sprawled there, the door rasped as it closed behind them, plunging them into darkness, choking with the nauseating stench that enveloped them cloggingly.

There were loud metallic noises as the hasp of the wagon door was closed and padlocked. Marion whimpered piteously. From the darkness a comforting arm reached out and encircled her shoulders.

"It's gonna be all right, honey," said Doris. "It's gonna be okay."

CHAPTER FOUR

As their eyes became accustomed to the gloom, they could make out the white blur of faces. A little daylight strained through a crack in the door and faces moved in towards them, hands reached out, touched them investigatingly. A torrent of questions in a dozen different languages fired at them.

The two girls shrank back against the door of the wagon. There was filth and disease around them, the air warm and heavy with the stench of decay and human excrement. They shuddered at what little they could see of their new companions; thick, matted hair, deep-sunk eyes and grimed faces. Marion pressed tightly against Doris, who kept her arms around her protectively. It was Doris who, masking her disgust, asked loudly: "Does anyone here speak German?"

A thin reedy voice came out of the darkness. "Ja. I speak German. A leetle."

"Where are you? I can't see you."

The crowd that hemmed them in, thrust and swayed. As they moved, the air thickened with their animal smell. A blurred face, almost indistinguishable from the others in the gloom, thrust towards her. "I speek Jerman," shrilled the voice again, and fetid, evil-smelling breath fanned Doris's cheeks as the woman cackled crazily.

"What are you doing here?" asked Doris. "Where are we going?"

"Where we go?" echoed the woman. She cackled again. "We nod know."

"How long have you been here?"

Another cackle. "Maybe tree, four weeks. I nod know."

Doris's brain reeled. Three or four weeks in this cattle truck? It was incredible. "We've got to get out of here," she burst out. "We've got to get out, somehow."

The woman said, "We go on. We come back. We go no place. We stay here. We here until die."

"Where d'you all come from?" persisted Doris.

The woman cackled again. This time it was clear to tell she was half-crazed. "We liff together long time. We come nowhere. Go nowhere."

"Were you sentenced to imprisonment?"

"Go nowhere," repeated the woman. Another cackle. "Hungry but go nowhere. Make yourself comfortable. Room for everybody." Another cackle. She pointed with a long, thin arm towards the far corner of the wagon. "Don't sit in that corner." She cackled again. "Nobody goes dat corner. Only for business."

"But this is crazy," protested Doris. "You must know why you're here, where you're going."

The woman was muttering to herself crazily, breaking into that shrill, half-crazed cackle. It was suddenly as though she'd forgotten Doris, pushed away from them into the gloom of the wagon. Then, startlingly, the sudden cry of a baby penetrated the darkness. They subsequently discovered the baby had been born a week earlier.

Marion whispered: "What does it mean? What is it all about?"

Doris said quietly: "In America we heard stories. Concentration camps where political prisoners are detained. Maybe that's where they're taking us."

"It's horrible, horrible," shuddered Marion.

A little later, ashamed of herself, she said to Doris: "I must get clean. I must change my clothes."

"You'll have to wait, honey," said Doris. "Wait until they let us out."

"But you don't understand. I thought we were going to be shot. I was terribly afraid." She broke off, then confessed weakly. "I was so scared, I lost control of myself, wet myself like a baby."

They were the same age, Doris suffering the same fears and worries as Marion. Yet it was Doris who comforted Marion, soothed her, tried to quiet her fears and ease her discomforts.

Hours later there was a sudden sharp shunting of the wagons. Buffers clanged, wagons jolted, metal wheels skidded on the rails, and with a slow, bumping movement, the train was moving.

There was a loud chorus of comments from the unseen women in the wagon and then slowly silence descended, punctuated by the wailing of the baby and muttered conversation in strange tongues from the darkness.

All day long and into the night, the wagon jolted slowly and noisily, sometimes halting for what seemed an eternity, then once again jolting into movement. There wasn't enough room for all of them to lie out and sleep. They squatted, hunched against each other, dozing, grunting and all the time breathing in and adding to the foul, thick air.

The following day when the wagon stopped, none of them had eaten or drunk. With some uncanny sense, the occupants of the wagon seemed to realise this stop was different from the others. There was an excited chattering of voices, shrill arguments and finally one woman shouldered her way to the door, stood waiting like a dog hoping to be let off the lead.

Once again the halt seemed interminable. When everyone was silent, jack-boots could be heard grinding the gravel in slow, measured paces.

Finally came the sound of the door being unlocked and, as it rolled back, bright sunlight flooded in on them, blinding them momentarily.

There was a panting crush now, faces eagerly strained towards the partly-opened door, drinking in the fresh air and the light of day.

The German guards outside pointed their guns menacingly, wrinkling their noses against the stench that flooded out towards them. A German officer gasped a question, and the woman who had previously shouldered her way through the crowd stepped forward eagerly, pathetically awaiting the nod of consent from the officer.

As she clambered from the wagon, dropped on to the gravel, Doris got her first good look at her, and shuddered. It was impossible to judge her age. She could have been thirty and once good-looking. Now she was emaciated beyond human belief. The dress she wore had been a white summery dress. Now it was a soiled, filthy garment that hung loosely around her, revealed the skinniness of her arms and legs, which seemed barely capable of supporting her weight.

There was a pathetic eagerness in her as, obeying the officer's pointing finger, she scrambled down the embankment towards a narrow, winding stream. Other women from other wagons were scrambling down towards the stream, carrying metal buckets and labouring up the embankment again, having filled them.

There was little strength left in the emaciated woman. She barely made it. But when Doris would have assisted her, one of the German soldiers bared his teeth, made menacing gestures with his rifle.

Weeks of confinement in that wagon under terrible conditions had resulted in some kind of order among the women. That one bucket of water was all allowed them. They each took it in turn to dip cupped hands into the bucket, scoop water to their mouths and gulp it greedily. Although they were parched, neither of the girls drank. The filthy condition of the other women was unbelievable. They dipped soiled hands into the water, scooped it to their lips and, as the water in the bucket became lower, so it became muddied, defiled by their hands.

The water-carrier, obeying another brief instruction, stumbled towards the end of the train in the wake of a tall, well-fed, rosy-cheeked German soldier. Later she returned escorted by him, her back bowed beneath a sack. She spilled the contents of the sack on to the wagon floor, and loaves of almost uneatable bread rolled across the floor. They were jumped on eagerly, torn in pieces by black, claw-like hands, chewed ravenously. Doris and Marion watched with loathing and pity deep down inside them.

But already their mouths were dry, their tongues swollen and the pain of hunger was in their own bellies. They looked on in horror and saw what they themselves would become in a matter of time.

Little time was allowed for eating. Once again the wagon doors were closed, followed by a long wait in the hot wagon before the wheels began to turn again.

Hunger and thirst are the masters of all men. Three days later, Marion and Doris were as eager for their rations as the others. Doris was the water-carrier one day and, being young and strong, was able to fill the bucket, carry it to the wagon without spilling. It was argued that being strong, she should always get it. But then there were others who too wanted their chance of a few minutes' walk in the open air.

One night, the mother of the baby died, and the train didn't stop for thirty-six hours. The smell of death was with them all that time. Now there was nobody to take care of the baby, and it cried interminably. Later the baby died too. Whether it died of starvation, or by being smothered by someone who could no longer bear to hear the agonising cries of the starving child, didn't seem important.

Living became dull, tortured existence, an everlasting waiting in the darkness until the wonderful moment when the doors opened and water and bread became available.

Time became unimportant. Only the opening of the doors became life. It might have been seven, seventy or seven hundred days before the train reached the end of its journey. Neither Doris nor Marion knew or cared.

CHAPTER FIVE

Dawn was breaking as the wagon doors slid open for the last time. It was raining hard, the half-light grey and cold, the German guards well-wrapped in their greatcoats.

But the physical discomfort of the weather was as nothing when the German officer shouted those magic words: "All out."

Unbelievably, they had reached the end of the trail. The swaying, endless jarring of the wagon had become so much a part of their lives, they felt themselves part of the wagon. It was almost unbelievably wonderful freedom as cramped, weakened and emaciated women painfully clambered from the wagon, dropped to the gravel and lined up in fours between the guards.

The train stood in a siding in the open country. Three of the wagon doors stood wide open, their occupants scrambling out into the open air of freedom. Doris's wagon was the fourth and, as they were herded down the embankment and along a rough track through tall pine trees, other guards moved to the fifth wagon, began to open it.

The rain poured down remorselessly, soaking them to the skin, chilling them in a matter of minutes. But after the long confinement in the filth of that wagon, the rain was sweet, refreshing and cleansing. The sweet smell of the pine trees was heavenly perfume and the soft carpet of pine needles beneath their feet like a feather bed.

Most of the women in Doris's contingent were in a bad way. They were weak from lack of food, cramped and barely able to walk after the weeks they'd spent in the wagon. There were nearly forty of them, stumbling weakly, the weak helping those who were weaker, and all the time the German guards growling at them, spurring them on with their rifle butts.

With almost animal relief, the release from the wagon drove all misgivings and conjectures from their minds. Where they were going or what would happen to them, did not matter. Instead, they turned their faces upwards to the rain, luxuriated as it washed them clean. Doris and Marion rubbed their faces and hands, felt thankfulness as some of the coating of dirt melted away.

They hadn't far to go. Not more than a quarter of a mile through the pine trees brought them to a stone building with high walls. So cleverly and carefully concealed was this building, from the outside, no-one even dreamt of its vastness.

41

There were SS guards outside. As the contingent approached, they unlocked a door in the wall, motioned the stumbling, weakened women inside.

Doris and Marion were young and strong, having spent far less time in the wagon than the rest of the women in their contingent. They were in front of the others, were the first to pass through the door into the quadrangle beyond.

It was a bare, stone quadrangle, quite small, with high walls probing upwards to the open sky. Already it was half-filled by the previous contingents, women of all ages, alike with their emaciation, haggard, tortured faces and burning eyes.

Doris was thinking quickly. There was no doubt in her mind now this was an internment or concentration camp. The stern rigours of the journey had already been suffered by them. Now started the real imprisonment. But they were both tired and exhausted. Sleep, food and rest were what they needed. The sooner they passed through reception, and the sooner they were allocated a cell, the easier it would be for them.

Apart from the door through which they'd just entered, there was only one other door. Doris took Marion by the arm, urged her, pushed through the other women, until they were both standing with their backs to this second door.

"Get it over quickly," said Doris. "It's the best thing."

Marion wasn't listening. She was staring at a girl only a few paces from them. This girl had obviously not arrived on the train. She had probably been brought a little earlier and by car. She was dressed like she was ready to shop in Fifth Avenue, high-heeled shoes, a smart hat and coat, expensive blouse and skirt, and protecting herself against the rain with an obviously new umbrella. She had long, silvery hair that rolled in waves to her shoulders, expensive rings on her fingers and three rows of pearls looped around her neck. She stood watching the women around her with undisguised loathing and contempt in her eyes. It was understandable. Even the steady downpour of rain could not wash away the soil and filth in which these women had lived for so many weeks.

"I wonder what she's doing here," said Marion.

"If it comes to that," said Doris, "what are we doing here?"

The door opened, another contingent of women were ushered inside. Everyone had to move over. Some women who, despite the rain-puddled concrete, had sunk into a sitting position, were forced to climb to their feet to make room for them. The fair-haired girl had to give way, shuddered with revulsion as she found herself thrust against Doris.

"Where is this?" Doris asked her.

The girl looked at her with loathing, said something bitingly in a strange tongue.

"I think it's Polish," said Marion.

The fair girl looked at her quickly, eyes widening slightly. She pointed at Marion, raised her eyebrows interrogatively. "American?"

Marion nodded.

"Me too," said Doris.

"Speek German?"

"Do you know where we are?" asked Doris in that language.

The girl shook her head. "Liddle German," she admitted. "Here Poland." She pointed to herself. "Name, Anna."

Once again the doors opened. It was a larger contingent this time. The quadrangle was becoming overcrowded and, to make room, the SS men at the far end were using their boots and fists. There was a sudden, surging crush of movement. Anna was jammed against the door. Anna's umbrella was knocked from her hand, was wafted away upon a sea of upturned faces and waving arms. Her face crinkled with revulsion as she found herself forcibly in contact with those around her. And now the rain was beating down, soaking her hair, dulling its lustre and threatening to straighten its shining waves. It was a tragedy for her. Tears gleamed in her eyes as her beautiful tresses began to spoil.

Doris and Marion tried to talk to her. But she had only a few words of German, and her serious concern with her clothes and her hair blinded her to everything else.

More contingents were brought along. Somehow, incredibly, they were packed inside. They were crammed so tight it was impossible to move their arms. Women groaned with the pain of crushed ribs, others fainted, remained on their feet, jammed too tightly to slip to the ground. And when it seemed that it was impossible for even one more emaciated woman to enter, still another contingent was forced in with them.

The last contingent was crammed in an hour after the trek from the wagons had begun. It stopped raining about the same time. The morning sun came out, hot and blazing, beating down on the thickly packed mass of humanity that panted and groaned breathlessly, so closely packed it moved as one unit. The hot sun drew the moisture from their sodden garments, drying them rapidly so the acrid smell of sweat mingled with a hundred other smells.

Crushed, barely able to move a finger, cramped so tightly they inhaled each other's breath, they sweated and suffered.

Midday the previous day was the last time they'd received anything to eat or drink, and now thirst came to torture them. Anna's face was red and her breath cramped in her body. But her wide eyes still tried to inspect her long, waving hair despairingly. You could read the hope in her eyes. Maybe it wouldn't lose its waves, maybe it would still retain its shining lustre.

The time passed in crushed, muffled, wheezing silence. Hour after hour, it seemed, marched past as they suffered and sweated. Doris was wearing a blue woollen jumper and a thick skirt. She was almost as damp now with perspiration, as previously she'd been with the rain. It dewed her forehead, trickled into her eyes, and she couldn't raise a hand to wipe it away. Her clothing enveloped her like a hot, damp blanket, suffocated her so she could hardly breathe, and the perspiration trickling down between her breasts, tingled and irritated unbearably.

The suffering was unending, enduring without end. And then, like the clear splash of cool water to a man in a blazing desert, they heard the sound of bolts being drawn the other side of the door against which they were pressed.

Doris gasped. "It won't be long now. Keep close behind me."

Marion squeezed her arm tightly. "We'll try to share the same cell," she gasped.

The door opened, just a little. It was on a chain. Otherwise the pressure against the door would have burst it inwards. A uniformed SS man stared with hard grey eyes, spoke to Doris. "You first," he said.

It was an effort. The door wasn't opened much and it was difficult for Doris to edge her way underneath the chain. Marion would have followed, but the SS man gestured at her fiercely, put his shoulder to the door, managed to force it closed.

Doris gasped with relief, eased from the crushing pressure, then looked around uneasily. She was in a long, cool, stone-walled room. To the left of her, two armed SS guards lounged against the wall smoking. To the right of her was a long table behind which were seated two more SS men. One of them glanced at her, indicated wordlessly she was to stand in front of the table.

It was so cool in there, so quiet, so fresh and clean, she almost fainted with the relief of it. The SS man had a virgin white blotter in front of him, a stack of unused printed record cards and a vase of flowers. On the wall behind him was a clock which showed it was two minutes past nine. With a shock, she realised that what had seemed to be a day of suffering was, for this man, the beginning of a normal day's work.

It was quiet in that room, so quiet she became nervous, watched him anxiously and a little afraid as he fitted a new nib to his pen, placed his inkwell nearer to hand. Further along the same table, the other SS man was arranging two stacks of envelopes.

Brown manila envelopes, one stack small-size and the other stack large. Behind him gaped the mouth of a chute. The kind of chute used in post offices.

The SS man took a blank record card, poised his pen and asked without looking at her: "Name?"

"Doris Langham."

He paused, looked at her with hard blue eyes. Impulsively she leaned forward across the table. "There's been a mistake, I'm sure," she said quickly. "I'm American. And if this is Poland ..."

He jerked back in his chair and his nose crinkled. She realised with a flush that the smell of her sickened him. He motioned her away with his hand, and embarrassedly she stepped back a pace. He motioned again. She stepped back another pace.

He said in clipped English: "You are American?"

"That's right."

He entered it on the record card, asked she should spell her name.

He had all the time in the world. He was unhurried, unflurried, entering the details accurately and carefully. With typical German precision, every vital piece of information was recorded: her father's name, her address in America, her age, her profession and so on.

Doris thought of the other women waiting outside, waiting while this cold, inhuman man completed his records, oblivious to their suffering and that they waited patiently hour after hour to appear before him.

"Crime charged with?"

She told him. Told him she had no right to be in Poland, that it was all a mistake. That the trial had been a travesty of justice.

He cut her short, wrote one word on the record card, pronounced it aloud for her benefit. "Espionage!"

She sighed. It was useless to argue. Only Marion's father could help. Until help came, she must suffer, bear everything with a stout heart.

"You have gold?" he asked.

"No," she replied. But his pointing finger and expression told her he wanted her jewellery. "Give," he instructed, holding out his hand.

She hesitated.

"All written down," he said in clipped English. "All returned when you leave."

Reluctantly she took off her wristwatch, her rings, earrings and diamond brooch. The other SS man reached across the table, took them from her. He spread them out, itemised them loudly, and as he did so they were neatly entered on her record card. The second man scooped them up, dropped them into a small manila envelope, sealed it carefully, referred to the record card and wrote on the envelope a long number.

The first man, without looking at her, said something she didn't understand. She stared at him.

His hard blue eyes looked at her. His mind fumbled for the English words, failed to find them. He pointed first at her blouse and then at her skirt. "Take off," he said.

Once again she hesitated.

"Take off," he rapped again, and his face was angry, impatient with her stupidity.

There was a hardness and disinterest about his manner which made it easier. Nevertheless, a flush stained her cheeks as she pulled her jumper over her head, realised it was damp with sweat and still clinging to her. The second man reached across and took the blouse from her. Self-consciously she loosened her skirt, let it slip around her ankles. When she straightened up with the skirt, the second man was reaching for it, her blouse already folded in front of him. "One blouse," he called.

"One blouse," echoed the first man, noting it on the record card.

"One skirt."

"One skirt," came the echo.

Her cheeks were blazing now. Her slip reached half way to her knees, was badly soiled. In the past days there had been no opportunity to wash or change her underclothing. She was acutely ashamed it should be seen by the eyes of men.

The first man was looking at her again, the skin over his cheekbones hardening in annoyance. He gestured with his hands. "Take off," he rapped. "Take off all. All!"

For a moment she froze with horror. To strip herself in front of them? It was unthinkable. But even as she squared her shoulders, held her head defiantly, she instinctively realised that to these impersonal men it was routine, the impersonal recording of cattle and possessions.

"Take off," he rapped again impatiently and, understanding the opposition in her squared shoulders and flushed cheeks, stared over her shoulder, snapped his fingers.

She glanced around terrified, saw the two SS men at the other side of the room straighten up at his summons. In a flash she understood their presence there, realised the uselessness and humiliation of being handled by them.

"Please," she said quickly. "I'll do it myself."

He waved his hand in dismissal. The SS guards returned to the wall, lounged against it impersonally, hard eyes watching her without interest.

46

She bent over, took the hem of her slip between her fingers, pulled it over her head.

"One slip," intoned the man who took it from her.

"One slip," came the echo as it was marked on her card.

Her whole body was bathed in ashamed flush.

"One brassiere!"

"One pair of shoes."

"One pair of knickers."

She stood shamed and humbled, completely naked, knees pressed tightly together in modesty, and forearm held across her breasts. She flashed a quick, shamed glance across the room at the SS men. They were staring at her, talking laughingly to each other in undertones. She stood motionless, sheltering her nakedness as much as she was able, waiting for the prison garments they would give her in place of her own.

Her clothing was thrust into one of the large manila envelopes. The envelope containing her jewellery thrust in with it. The envelope was sealed down, neatly labelled with a long number. The envelope was dropped into the chute to slip out of sight.

The first man neatly blotted the record card, read it through slowly and carefully. Then he reached across the desk, handed it to her. His finger pointed to the far end of the room. "That door," he said.

She looked along the room with shame flushing her cheeks anew. It was a long walk. And every inch of the way ...

"That door," he rasped again.

From the corner of her eye she caught a flicker of movement from the SS guards. Anything was better than they should touch her. She started walking, taking small paces, crouching slightly, acutely conscious that mocking eyes were absorbing every movement of her quivering haunches.

It was a swing door. When she got near it she heard the guards laughing, quickened her pace, thrust through the swing door almost at a run.

The room beyond was long and wide. Two uniformed SS men lounging against the wall glanced up mildly surprised. She stopped short, hands instinctively covering herself as once again she acutely realised her nakedness. But their manner and eyes were so uninterested she was able to brace herself, following their pointing fingers.

There was a wooden armchair in the centre of the room, two white-coated men standing beside it, deep in conversation. One turned his head as she timidly approached, barely glanced at her, went on talking to his companion while he extended his had towards her.

47

She understood what he wanted, handed him the record card. He took it, continued his discussion while she stood there with beating heart, hands protectively clasped over her breasts.

Strangely enough their attitude helped her. As a woman she was insulted by their indifference. But as a stripped and naked woman she was thankful for their indifference.

The man who had taken her record card closed the conversation on a note of interrogation, crossed the room to a far corner without another glance at her. The second man, without looking at her, gestured towards the chair. She was to sit down.

She sat on the edge of it timidly, noticing that it was solidly built and screwed to the floor, festooned with leather straps. He said something and when she didn't respond or understand he thrust at her shoulder, pushed he back into the chair, bent over her and was buckling a strap tightly around her waist before she realized what was happening.

His fingers held ready a strap on the arm of the chair. He said something and once again was impatient with her lack of understanding, seized her arm, dragged it from her breast and firmly clamped it to the arm of the chair.

The fear rose strongly inside her. The tethering of her body and arm forced upon her realization of her helplessness in the hands of these men. She squirmed, resisted violently when he tried to strap her other arm. He was rough with her, wrenched her arm painfully, strapped it tightly so the leather bit deep into her flesh. Defenceless now, she felt her nakedness more acutely, whimpered and writhed in the chair. Her struggles increased his annoyance, caused him to tighten even more the strap around her waist so it cut painfully into the soft skin of her belly.

The other man was returning now, trundling a gleaming, chromium-plated trolley. With the detachment of an architect preparing his drawing instruments, he picked a gleaming cylinder tipped with a sharply-pointed needle and attached it to a long length of flex. She stared with wide, fear-crazed eyes, her heart pounding and wild conjecture flooding through her. When he approached her, she strained uselessly to escape her pinions. Then as the needle poised over her arm she turned her head away with a sob of fear, convinced she was to be anaesthetised in preparation for some inhuman experiment.

The stab of the needle in her arm was red-hot, so that her muscles contracted, trying to escape the pain. But the tightly-drawn straps held her arm firmly and the needle jabbed again and again, stabbing fire into her flesh so she panted with the sharp hurt of it. Then as it continued, she had to look, turned her head to stare with unbelieving eyes at the record card number being indelibly etched into her flesh, the stabbing tattoo needle penetrating the skin, tracing a pattern that could never be removed.

She stared, whimpered. The needle was electric, stabbed painfully and rhythmically. Her white skin was reddened and swollen now, the ink pattern a deep black.

He finished the number, fastidiously sterilized the point of the needle with ether-soaked cotton-wool. The other man wiped tiny beads of blood from her arm, carefully cleansed the section with disinfected cotton-wool. He stared critically at the tattooed number, nodded his head approvingly and dipped his hand into his overall pockets as he moved around back of Doris.

She caught a glimpse of shining metal gleaming as he withdrew his hand from his pocket. But he was behind her. She tensed, bracing herself against the back of the chair, preparing for what might come next. His fingers locked in her hair, her head was strained back as he tugged hard. Then came a soft scrunching noise and the sharp snip of scissors.

She felt the soft touch of falling hair on her bare shoulders and went crazy at the thought of what they were doing now. She writhed, screamed, twisted and jerked her head in protest. One wrapped his arm around her neck, half-choking her, holding her head as though in a vice. She heard the busy snip, snip, snip of the scissors and felt her luxuriant hair falling in handfuls. All she had been through she could endure again, but this ... this final desecration!

But the arm held her head remorselessly, the snipping continued until with dumb realization she knew her hair had been cropped short. She was numbed, crying soundlessly when the scissors were exchanged for clippers and run again and again across her skull, shaving her clean to the scalp.

When they released her head she sat there limply, silent tears rolling down her cheeks and clipped hair covering her shoulders. They released her and she still sat there silently crying. One of them took her wrists, pulled her to her feet roughly, gestured towards a door at the far end of the room. Forgotten was her nakedness and the indignity of being numbered; all her miseries were engulfed by this final shame of being hairless, shaved to the bone. Unseeingly she stumbled to the door, was barely conscious of the SS man who pushed it open for her, bolted it behind her.

She was in another room, empty of furniture and windowless. The light strained through a fanlight in the roof. The door at the far end was locked and dimly she realized that she was intended to remain here.

She put her fingers to her head, was shocked anew by the unaccustomed feel of her cropped skull. Physically and mentally exhausted she sank down on her haunches, bare flesh against stone floor, and cried silently.

But Doris was tough. Much tougher than Marion. And during the next few minutes she realized she must somehow find the strength to help and encourage her friend. Thus it was that when, ten minutes later, Marion too stumbled into the room, humiliated, naked and shorn, Doris was able to suppress her shudder of horror and comfort Marion.

The third girl was Anna. They didn't recognize her at first, naked and without her lustrous, gleaming, shoulder-length hair. She wasn't crying. There was a numbed, shocked expression in her eyes, as though she couldn't yet believe it had happened. She looked grotesque, her bald head gleaming, incredibly small, much too small for her wide black eyes. Her clothes too had skillfully concealed her figure. Although her legs were long and shapely, ribs stood out starkly and her breasts were large but flat, sagging heavily. No one would have recognized now the smartly dressed, luxuriant beauty, who had but a short time before, stood outside with her nose wrinkled in disgust at the folk around her.

"How do I look?" asked Doris, with an attempt at cheerfulness.

Marion stared at her, eyes filled with piteous hurt. "You don't ... look the same."

Marion didn't look the same either. But Doris didn't say so. Somewhere, somehow, she found the courage to work up a smile. "We all start from scratch anyway," she said. "Nobody has any advantages over the others." She smiled ruefully. "Not even clothes!"

It was the knowledge they were not alone that helped. As, one after the other, women came through that door, naked and hairless, old women, young women, fat women, emaciated women, the knowledge they were all suffering the same hardships, gave them new strength. Doris even began to make Marion smile by passing comments about the tearful newcomers who stumbled through the door away from the horror of the shearing room.

Almost fifty naked women were crammed into that small room by the time the other door was opened. It opened on to a courtyard. Bright sunlight blazed down on them as, obeying the guard's instructions, they stepped out into the open in single file. Anna was in front, Doris followed with Marion behind.

The courtyard was long and narrow, leading to a timber-built hut at the far end. Instinctively Doris realized it was lunch time and the idle SS men standing around were here to be amused. But it could not have been for their sensual pleasure, because this pathetic file of hairless, humiliated women was a tragic, pitiful sight.

Halfway to the hut was a small tank of pungent smelling liquid. Beside it was the first inmate of the prison they had seen. She might have been a young woman. But suffering had so lined her face it was difficult to judge her age. She wore a single, sack-like garment that reached halfway to her knees. On her right hand she wore an elbow-length rubber glove.

The guard barked an order at Anna, who stood at the head of the column. Anna timidly stepped forward, stood with legs astride beside the tank. The woman stooped wearily, fished around in the tank with her gloved hand, came up with a dripping sponge. The guard snapped another order. Anna raised her arm and the woman applied the sponge to her armpit, swabbing so thoroughly the liquid ran down Anna's side and trickled off her flanks.

The guard barked another order. Anna dropped her arm, raised her other. The woman soaked the sponge, applied it.

A third time the woman soaked the sponge, this time applied it to Anna's body, swabbed thoroughly.

The SS men standing around watching, chuckled expectantly. The guard motioned and Anna set off towards the hut. Doris was next in line; shamefacedly she stepped forward, stood with feet astride beside the tank.

Doris approved of this routine. During her imprisonment in the wagon, one of her greatest torments were the lice she had picked up. The separation of prisoners from their clothes and this baptism in disinfectant, showed cleanliness would be one of the minor advantages to offset the other miseries.

She knew what was wanted, raised her arm without being ordered. The loaded sponge was cold and searching, the disinfectant strong and burning. She watched the woman as she wearily stooped, soaked the sponge a second time before she applied it. Vaguely she wondered how many times this woman had performed this same operation.

As the woman soaked the sponge for the third time, Doris was grateful this task had not been entrusted to a man. It would have been too much. The loaded sponge was applied to her body, swabbed searchingly. Then, dripping, she obeyed the guard's gesture, walked towards the hut.

She was the centre of attention now, every SS man, it seemed, watching her intently. It seemed a lifetime since she'd arrived here, a lifetime since she'd parted with her clothes and hair. She was no longer conscious of her nakedness or shaven head. She was just one among so many cattle. She held herself erect, walked with dignity and at the same time became conscious of the rapidly increasing, burning sensation.

That disinfectant was strong, probably undiluted. It had been applied to the most sensitive parts of her body. Soft, delicate membranes were smarting more and more beneath the irritating, scorching burn of disinfectant.

She faltered in her step with the smart of it, half-bent with the sharp sting of it and, as a chorus of chuckles sounded from the eagerly watching SS men, she understood why they were waiting so expectantly.

She forced herself to remain erect, forced herself to walk slowly. But the sharp sting of it became unbearable so she hurried her pace. Then with brutal laughs echoing around her she gave way to the smarting agony, burst into a run, sought shelter in the hut, holding herself to ease the pain, before she realized two other grinning SS men were waiting there, savouring her torment.

For a moment her smarting was too great for her to heed them. Then, gritting her teeth, she once again held her head erect, stared at them defiantly.

One of them, grinning broadly, gestured towards another inmate of the prison who sat behind a counter. As Doris approached she wearily pulled a sack-like garment from the rack behind her, set it down on the counter for Doris to take, motioned towards the open door at the far end.

Doris was still in agony. She took the garment, hurried from the mocking grins of the SS men into the open air at the far end.

A series of guards irregularly spaced formed a long avenue towards one of many distant huts. Instinctively she knew the end of her humiliations was in sight. There wasn't much else that could be done to her now.

Now, as she stumbled towards the hut, naked, shamed and smarting, a target for the eyes of all men, she felt nothing. She was dead inside. Just dead.

The hut was built of solid timber, with small iron gratings for windows and a corrugated-iron roof. It was long and narrow, flanked on both sides with three-tier bunks, a small avenue to walk between them. Anna was gazing around stupidly when Doris arrived. Each bunk had a dirty straw-filled mattress and a filthy blanket. Doris glanced at the blankets and her heart dropped. The formality of being cleansed with disinfectant was a farce. The blankets and mattresses were alive with lice. She could see them with her naked eyes. And when she looked at the garment supplied her she could see that too was verminous.

But even that garment was preferable to the searching eyes of strange men probing her naked body. She shook it out, examined it. It was like a long sack, the bottom cut away for her head to enter and the corners cut away for her arms. When with a shudder she pulled it over shoulders, it was harsh to her soft skin, reached half way to her knees, rasped painfully across her tautly thrusting breasts.

Anna still wore that numbed look in her eyes. She stared at Doris, numbly copied her. Her garment was short. So short it made her limbs seem even longer and spindly. She looked so much like a cartoon flour bag on two spindly legs that Doris laughed.

Marion came in then, caught sight of Anna and despite herself laughed also. From that moment onwards developed the spirit that sustained them through the coming months; an ability to find humour in small things and to laugh despite their tribulations.

It was hot in that shed. The tiny gratings allowed in little air and the hot sun beating on the iron roof turned it into an oven. As more and more women entered the hut, climbed into the sack-like garments, it became obvious there would be a shortage of bunks. Marion and Doris selected bunks one above the other, lay on them thankfully in the stifling heat and wondered when they would eat. It was a continual procession. All day long a steady procession of naked, hairless women of all ages entered the hut. Soon there were so many there was only room for them two on a bunk.

Finally they were three on a bunk, half-sitting, half-lying on each other, sweating and suffocating in the baked, oven-like atmosphere. All of them were ravenous and gasping for a cooling drink. Almost thirty-six hours had passed since they'd last eaten. And then they'd eaten very little. They were almost despairing of eating at all when the door of the hut opened, armed guards appeared and they were marched across a brightly lighted plateau to a larger hut.

Each woman collected two panikins. One was for water and the other for food. The water was cold, strongly tainted with chlorine. But it was gulped down eagerly. The food was tasteless, boiled potatoes and black bread. But that was eaten ravenously. Then they were marched back to their hut, herded inside and the doors locked on them.

There was no light. In the darkness they pushed and squeezed each other, huddled themselves three on a bunk, tried to rest and get warmth from the single blanket that went to each bunk.

Doris went to sleep with Marion cuddled in her protective embrace. Another woman lay half-sprawled across them, her bare feet within inches of Doris's nose. During the night the woman in the bunk above was violently sick. But even if there'd been light, there was no water to clean up with. Conditions were so cramped it was impossible to do anything about it.

It had been a lifetime of misery but only the first day of many in that camp.

CHAPTER SIX

Marion moved and Doris suddenly broke off talking.

"She's getting out of bed," she said breathlessly. She got up hurriedly and ran through to the bedroom. I caught a glimpse of Marion before Doris discreetly closed the door. That same staring look was in her eyes and she'd got straight up out of bed, her small compact breasts firm and naked.

I poured myself another drink. Listening to Doris had transported me to a grim, hard world of the past which even now I found it difficult to believe had ever existed. During the war and after, stories of concentration camps had been widespread. Even with the publicity given to Belsen and the actual photographs of these atrocities, it was still difficult to believe it could happen.

And sitting here in this flat in Chicago, listening to Doris quietly talking, telling what happened to her, proving it with the tattooed number on her arm, still found me almost unable to believe these things had happened.

I guess that's that way it is for most folks. Such inhumanity cannot even be imagined by ordinary folks. It's so far from their minds, they can't even believe that other folk can behave with such brutality.

I guess the real reason is that ordinary folks are too decent. Ordinary folks don't want wars, they don't want brutality and they don't want Governments riding on their backs on the time. What ordinary folk want is peace, to live a quiet, decent life and the less interference from the Government the better.

But it isn't the ordinary folks who run the world. The ordinary folk are too decent to want to organise or push anyone around.

It's the misfits, the egotists, the power-conscious politicians and vainglorious tub-thumping talkers who spoil the world for everyone else.

It was in Germany that the misfits and the vain egotists seeking self-glory started the armaments race, pushing around the man in the street until, in order to maintain their power, they finally devised the concentration camp.

But I guess it's the same the world over. It isn't the ordinary, decent man in the street who wants to fire a gun, drop a bomb or clap someone in jail or concentration camp. It's the Big Boys at the top who wanna do these things, the Big Boys who got where they are by shooting off their mouths, clambering on the shoulders of the little guys, exalting their position by mouthing useless phrases which are calculated to stir the ordinary, decent man into action.

These misfit politicians are the real menace of life today. The power-crazed politicians of *all* countries, who intone with mock sincerity in their Assembly-hall voices, the same old ringing demands. "Our social integrity." ... "The great Fatherland" ... "pride of our nation" ... "tradition of our forefathers" ... and so on. They use these phrases to persuade the ordinary, decent folk to achieve the blind, egotistical ambitions of the politicians.

Yeah. That's the way I get when I think about the world today. Good and mad! Because life could be so good for everyone. Yet all we see on the horizon is the mushroom of an exploding atom-bomb which we know when once let loose upon the world will destroy millions from radiation and wounds within a matter of days or weeks from the time the madness starts.

The bedroom door opened and Marion, now wearing a dressing-gown, came out like a sleep-walker, eyes staring expressionlessly in front of her. Doris gave me a wry smile, held Marion's arm. "Wants the bathroom," she explained with a shy flush.

I paced the room, scowled and thought of these two sweet dames, just kids, seventeen years of age, undergoing an experience that was branded as indelibly on their minds as their arms had been branded.

They came out from the bathroom. Doris steered Marion back to bed, tucked sheets up beneath her chin, and stood looking down at her.

I went into the bedroom, stood alongside Doris. Marion's eyes were closed now and she seemed to be sleeping. "Poor kid," I said.

Doris sighed. "I hope she's going to be all right."

"She'll be okay," I said confidently. I had no reason to be confident. But I felt any dame who'd been through what Marion had suffered wouldn't buckle easily.

Marion opened her eyes at that moment. She stared at the ceiling vacantly and then her head slowly turned, her eyes brushing across Doris's face, coming to rest upon mine.

For long seconds her eyes remained vacant. Then fear glimmered deep down in her pupils, rapidly possessed her until her face was contorted with wild and desperate terror. In a kinda crazy frenzy she threw herself off the bed, lunged for the bedside table.

It was so unexpected, she had the drawer open and her fingers around the gun butt before I could reach her. She was gonna use it. There wasn't any doubt of that. Her fingers were curling around the butt, index finger searching for the trigger as I went into action.

You couldn't horse around with a dame in that state. I chopped the edge of my palm across the back of her hand real hard. It hurt. She shrieked with the pain of it. She dropped the gun too.

Doris was scrambling for it while I was trying to hold down what seemed like seventeen furious tigresses. I got my face scratched, a knee in the groin, a small fist in my eye and a chunk bitten from my wrist, all in a few seconds.

It stopped as suddenly as it began. She went limp like a rag doll. I was suspicious at first, thought she was foxing. But it was genuine. She'd burned herself out and was in another faint.

Doris helped me tuck her up in the blankets. She looked like a little doll, breathing softly, face pale and black hair straggly against the white pillows.

I mopped my forehead, sucked my bleeding hand.

Doris excused her, saying: "She was delirious, didn't know what she was doing."

I didn't say anything. I picked up the revolver Doris had put on the bedside table, clicked open the cartridge chamber. It was fully loaded and the safety-catch was only half-on. It was a German make with an ornamented butt. Essentially a ladies' weapon but dangerous nonetheless.

"She always carries it around," said Doris quietly. "She doesn't feel safe without it. Gives her confidence. She's felt that way ever since ..." She broke off, stared at me with tragic eyes.

I weighed the gun in my hand, passed it to Doris. "Be smart," I said. "Tuck it away someplace she won't find it."

She clutched the gun, stared at me with worried yes. "I'm so sorry," she said penitently. "She's got a thing about men ever since ..."

"Skip it."

"You're so understanding, Hank," she said gratefully. I watched her tuck the gun away beneath laundered underclothes in a dresser drawer.

"That's not hiding it."

"I'll get rid of it later, Hank. I promise."

We left the bedroom door open, went back to the lounge. I lit a cigarette, offered one to Doris. She shook her head, wearily, tiredly. There were dark rings under her eyes.

"Is that where she had the first case of shock?" I asked. "In the concentration camp?"

She nodded.

"Right after you got there?"

She shook her head. Her face was hard and her eyes stared into the past. "No," she said quietly. "It was a long while later. Something happened."

"Tell me about it."

She looked at her watch and then up into my face. I could see the tiredness at the back of her eyes, realised what a strain it musta been for her to tell me about Poland. "It's good of you to stay," she said. "What about your rest?"

"Don't worry," I said. "I can sleep in the morning. I'm not working until tomorrow evening."

"I hope you won't think I'm not being sociable," she said wearily. "But you see ..."

"I know," I interrupted. "You're tired. You'd like to curl up."

She nodded, crinkled her nose in a smile. "D'you mind terribly?"

"You push off," I said. "I'll keep an eye on her. You won't have to worry."

"You're so kind."

She got up slowly, pressed her hand to her forehead like she had a headache and fluttered her eyelids. "Call me if she wakes," she said.

"I will."

"And call me anyway in four hours. I'll relieve you."

"Sure," I said. "I'll call you about four."

She went into her own bedroom. I lit another cigarette, poured myself another drink, glanced through some magazines. A little later she came out of her bedroom wearing an ankle-length negligee with a tightly-drawn girdle. Her black hair gleamed as it brushed her shoulders, and the liquid play of her haunches as she walked towards the bathroom got me interested.

And it made me flush with shame. Watching the roll and thrust of her buttocks beneath the negligee reminded me of the way those SS men must have watched her, made me feel mean, ashamed of myself.

When she came out of the bathroom her eyes were still tired. She came across to me, leaned over my shoulder so she could see what I was reading. A loop of hair brushed my cheek. "What are you reading?" she asked.

"The usual stuff," I growled. "An article on how just one hydrogen bomb can destroy the world and how the smart thing is to make as many of them as possible."

He hair was soft against my cheek, her breath hot on my neck, and the tantalising smell of perfume disturbing my senses. I turned my head so I could stare into her black, mischievous eyes. "D'you like atom bombs?"

"You know it, I know it," she chuckled. "The world's crazy." She shrugged her shoulders. "What can we do about it?"

I edged around some more. The way she was stooping caused the negligee to gape at the front. She musta known it. She stayed the way she was, bent over me, pretending to look at my magazine.

"You've seen it," I said. "You know what war really means."

I shifted around a little more. Now I could see the soft whiteness of her skin, the curved ripeness of them as they hung, pressing weightily against the negligee, which supported them and imparted to them mysterious, intriguing shadows. I was staring, fascinated and magnetised. She knew it, stayed the way she was so I could go on being magnetised. "I'm a woman," she said softly. "Women are more philosophical and earthy. They think more about the essential things of life."

"Such as?"

"Life and living."

I raised my gaze to her black eyes. They were smiling invitingly. I reached up, slipped my arm around her neck, pulled her lips down to mind. She responded eagerly, almost hungrily, and as she stooped even lower, her breasts spilled out, white, soft and weighty.

It only lasted a moment before she pulled herself away. Her face was flushed as she quickly adjusted her negligee, first one side and then the other. "You mustn't," she whispered excitedly. "You mustn't kiss me like that."

She wasn't stooping over me any more and she hadn't made a good job of readjusting the negligee. One breast was almost fully revealed. "What's biting you?" I asked. "Frightened you'll lose your teeth?"

Her cheeks flushed prettily and her eyes sparkled. "It's too soon, Hank," she said reprovingly. "Once you start, you never know where it ends and ... well we hardly know each other."

I was getting ready to know her. She musta known about that partially revealed breast. It lay quietly within the scanty confinement of her negligee, soft and inviting. It was the symbol of her essential femininity and disturbingly tempting.

"How long d'you have to know a guy before you shake hands?"

She chuckled. "You know how it is, Hank." She sighed. "I must go to bed now."

But she didn't. She still stood there and she must have liked me looking, because she didn't move and I was doing nothing else but.

"Well ..." she said at last. "I must go now."

"I could tuck you up in bed. I'm pretty good at it."

"Oh no," she said quickly. "That wouldn't do at all." She was careful not to move, so I could go on seeing her.

"Kiss you goodnight?"

"I'd like that," she said softly, and as I moved tentatively, added quickly: "But you'd better not. I'd rather you didn't."

I sank back with a sigh. "Looks like being a dull party."

"Have you really found it dull, Hank?"

She still hadn't moved. You know how it is with a guy, always ambitious and wanting more, never satisfied with what there is. "It was fine," I said. "But it could have been brighter."

"Don't rush me, Hank," she pleaded. "Don't rush me."

She moved then, and the soft whiteness slipped away. "Goodnight, Hank," she said tenderly. "There's always tomorrow."

"Goodnight, Doris." I watched her as she walked to the bedroom, this time not ashamed to notice the tightness of the negligee and the liquid movement of her haunches.

She closed the bedroom door and I resumed my reading of the article on atom bombs. But I was reading with only half my mind. The other half was thinking of a different type of atom bomb. White, soft, milky atom bombs that, when handled, surged with sudden life, radiated burning rays of intoxicating pleasure.

I flung the magazine on the settee, paced the room, chain-smoked cigarettes and drank half the bottle of whiskey. Marion slept peacefully all the time. I didn't know if Doris was sleeping. I hoped she wasn't. She hadn't any right to sleep. Not after disturbing my peace of mind this way.

Just the same, I didn't wake her at the end of four hours. I let her go on sleeping. Marion went on sleeping too. When the grey light of dawn began to penetrate the room, I was hollow-eyed, dry-tongued and headachy.

Doris awoke early, scolded me for not waking her to relieve me and went through to the kitchen to make some coffee. I went through to the kitchen with her. She was still wearing that negligee and it still gaped at the front. But after a sleepless night it didn't exert the same magnetism. She seemed to know it. "You must be tired," she said considerately. "Why not curl up in my bed for a while?"

"I need a shower," I said. "I need a shave and I need a change of clothes. I'd better go home. But thanks for the offer."

"Well, drink this coffee, first."

It was good coffee, hot and strong. It cleared my head. "I'd like to know how Marion makes out," I said.

"You'll ring, of course?"

I looked her over, slowly, lingeringly. She dropped her eyes, smiled secretly. "You didn't get through telling me about the concentration camp," I pointed out.

"You want to hear about it?"

"Sure I do."

"That's one excuse for meeting again," she chuckled.

She came to the door with me, leaned against the door post. "You've been very kind."

"But not very lucky," I said drily.

Her eyes danced mischievously and her mouth pursed impudently. "You're in such a hurry," she teased.

"You're the first dame to complain."

"Maybe you need a shower at that," she said. "A cold shower!"

It was a different elevator hop. He stared at me stonily, dropped the lift to the ground floor like he made regular parachute jumps and liked the feeling. I'd parked my car in the road outside the apartment block. A harness cop was leaning against it, thumbs in his belt. He grinned broadly as I tiredly walked towards him, fumbling in my pocket for the car key.

"Parked all night without a light, bud," he said with relish.

"Okay," I said tiredly. "Give it to me."

He took his time writing the summons. "Let's make a job of it while we're about it, fella," he said happily. "Now let me see. Parked without lights, dirty number plate not visible at twenty-five yards, back window dirty obstructing driver's view." He grinned at me. "Anything more you can think of?"

"Not right now," I said bitterly. "But I'll think up something on the way home; write and tell you."

He thrust the ticket in my hand, heaved a sigh of satisfaction. "You know how it is, bud. Just don't like to go back to headquarters empty-handed."

I scowled at him. "D'you mind if I get going now? Or will the noise of my engine disturb the peace?"

"Keep it up, fella," he said happily. "Pretty soon you'll start cussing. That's an offence too. Using obscene words and behaviour."

He automatically fumbled for his pencil, moistened his lips in readiness to wet the pencil point.

"You're a real credit to the force," I told him with heavy sarcasm. "Ordinary citizens like me feel safe with watch-dogs like you around."

"Just mention it to the judge, will you?" he said, cheerfully. "I could do with promotion."

I growled unpleasant words beneath my breath, started the engine, drove the car forward a coupla yards in preparation to reverse. I'd parked on the wrong side of the road and had to turn around.

He was at my driving window again, summons sheet out and pencil poised. "You've done it again, bud," he grinned.

"Done what?"

"Driving on the wrong side of the road," he said with relish, filling in the details.

I took the ticket, stuffed it angrily into my pocket.

"You won't forget to be in court, will ya?" he warned.

"I'll do better," I told him. "I'm going straight down the DA's office and tell him what a real smart cop you are."

"That's real nice of you, bud," he said approvingly. "That's real nice of you."

I took that shower when I got home, took it as hot as I could stand it; then I dried off, climbed into bed and was asleep as soon as my head hit the pillows. I wasn't due at the office until late afternoon. But there were always things cropping up. I can never rely on regular hours. It was best to get my sleep while I had the chance. And just for a moment as I relaxed on the soft mattress between the clean white sheets, I thought of Doris, remembered the days and nights she'd spent in that filthy, congested wagon.

Yeah, there were many consolations in living in Chicago. Even if traffic cops were getting in your hair all the time.

CHAPTER SEVEN

I got an assignment that same evening. Gus Morton, convicted murderer and jail-breaker, had been seen on the outskirts of Chicago. Road-blocks had been set up on all highways and the cops were working overtime to get him. He wasn't only a jail-breaker. He was a cop-killer too, and there wasn't a cop on the force who wasn't ready to work all hours, to put Gus behind bars again.

I got assigned to the job.

The Chief said: "You know the kinda thing I want, Hank. I don't want an eye-witness report written in some beer parlour on the strength of what some green cop tells you. I want a real eye-witness account. I want folks to read and feel they were actually there when it happened. Gus Morton's been a pain in everyone's neck. Everyone will want to know how the law finally caught up with him."

"You want I should take him myself?" I sneered.

His blue eyes gave me an up-and-under glance. He rolled his cigar from one corner of his mouth to the other. "That wouldn't surprise me neither," he said drily.

I used one of the *Chronicle*'s staff cars. I took Jerry Wilmot with me. He was our star photographer. If the Chief wanted an eye-witness report, the *Chronicle* readers might as well have a few close-ups of Gus shooting me full of holes while I got it.

The chase had spread further afield by evening. Gus had socked an old geezer with a brick, taken his car and used it as a jeep across open country. But the cops had him sewed up now, cordoned off in a twenty square mile area which they were steadily narrowing, using walkie-talkie radio, bloodhounds and every other man-hunt aid.

That evening me and Jerry sat playing poker in a cafe while the search continued. Nothing much could be done after dark except post cops as sentries and make sure Gus didn't break the cordon. Jerry cleaned me out of my last nickel. I borrowed back a coupla dimes and put through a call to Chicago.

"How's it going?" I asked.

"I've been trying to get you all day," she said eagerly.

"Marion's better?"

"Much better." Relief throbbed in her voice.

"What did the doctor say?"

"She's over it," she said. "She's got a headache. Apart from that, she's almost her normal self."

"Any idea what caused the shock?"

There was a pause. She said uncertainly: "We'll talk about that when I see you." A softer note came into her voice. "Are you coming along tonight?"

"Wish I could," I said glumly. "I'm stuck down here on a story."

"Will it be long, Hank?" she said wistfully.

"I don't know. Depends on how dumb the cops are and how smart Morton is."

"Come as soon as you can, won't you, Hank?"

I was remembering her the way she'd been last night, negligee gaping open and her eyes sparkling mischievously. "You bet," I said. "I'll be around first chance I get."

It was the only cafe for miles. Most of the other newshounds were there and it was gonna become a reporters' doss-house. A group of the boys were over by the hard drinks counter. They'd been there for the past coupla hours. Jenny Finton of the *Echo* was there too, drinking as hard as any of them. She was the only one still sober.

Jerry caught my eye meaningfully as I left the telephone box. I nodded, walked across to the counter. Momentarily Jenny's eyes caught mine, hardened with contempt, then glanced away. I flushed, felt myself wither to knee-height. The bartender caught my eye. "Two Scotch," I ordered.

Tony Evans of the *Sun* rapped loudly on the counter, said in a blurred voice: "I wanna drink."

The bartender's eye caught mine questioningly. I nodded agreement. Tony was in a boisterous mood that might turn aggressive at any moment. The bartender asked: "What kinda drink, fella?"

"Why, it's a ..." A puzzled look stole over his face. He swayed back on his heels, almost overbalanced.

"What kinda drink?" repeated the bartender.

"I'm tryin' remember," drawled Tony. He screwed his head around, said over his shoulder: "That's funny, fellas. Can't remember the name."

"Who'sh name," demanded Ron Regan and laughed uproariously. At the same time, he rested his arm on Jenny's shoulder, half-leaned on her. Coldly and distantly she detached herself.

Tony told the bartender: "Doan remember name. But it's ... it's ... tall, plenny cold and it'sh full of gin."

Ronald said truculently: "Hey. Hey! That's no way to talk about my girl."

"You shuddup," blurred Tony.

"Sure," said Ronald. "Sure. I ssshuddup." He looped his arm around Jenny's shoulder. "You ain't full o' gin, is you, honey?"

Carefully, distantly, she detached herself, eyed him hostilely. The bartender gave Tony a long drink in a tall glass, lots of ice and water and very little gin. He poured two whiskies for me and I carried them back to my table.

Jerry loaned me ten bucks out of the money he'd won from me and we continued playing.

It was warm in that cafe. We could get food and we could get drinks. That was all to be said for it. As a hotel it was lousy. The chairs were hard, the tables wooden.

Later on, Jerry and I spread our mackintoshes on the floor, sat with our backs against the wall and our fedoras sheltering our eyes from the harsh glare of the electric lights. It's part of a newspaper man's job to be prepared to sleep anywhere at any time.

A little later Jenny came over, stood staring down at us. The way I was sitting with my hat over my eyes, I could see only her feet. They were dainty feet, with neatly turned ankles. I pushed my hat on to my forehead with my forefinger, squinted up at her. She stared down at me hostilely without saying anything. I asked: "Still mad at me?"

"I could kill you," she said tonelessly.

"I'll tell you the way it was," I began.

"I don't want to talk about it," she snapped.

I stared at her. She stared back.

"Anything I can do for you?"

Slowly and deliberately she turned her head, stared across the cafe to where the other newshounds were lying on the floor asleep, sprawled across tables or still tipsily drinking.

She didn't say anything. But I saw in her face what was in her mind. I moved away from Jerry, spread my mackintosh and invited: "If your honour's at stake, we'll call a truce."

"It still doesn't mean I think you're any better than them," she warned. "It was one of the most despicable tricks ..."

"You don't want to talk about it," I reminded.

Her eyes flashed. "That's right," she snapped. "It was too despicable to discuss."

"Siddown," I invited. "Take a weight off your legs."

"And if it wasn't that they've been drinking too much and are not themselves ..."

"Siddown and shut up," I growled. "They're wolves and you know it. They have to be wolves to be in this racket."

She sat down with a flurry of skirts, pressed her shoulders against the wall, heaved a sigh and relaxed.

Jerry asked sleepily from beneath his fedora: "We got company, Hank?"

"Don't mind me do you, Jerry?" she said softly. Her voice was winning, coaxing. She was that way with him to make me mad.

"Don't take all the blankets," he mumbled.

"Here comes one wolf," I warned Jenny.

It was Tony. He'd been looking around for Jenny, suddenly realised she was missing. He staggered over to us, stood blearing down at Jenny. "Hello, honey," he said throatily.

She took my arm, fingers pinching tightly. "Let it ride, Hank," she whispered. "Don't make trouble."

"I'm cold, honey," he said petulantly. He rocked back on his heels, almost lost his balance, beat the air with his arms. "Le'us go some placsh where you keep me warm." He stooped, reached out for her, missed her shoulder by a coupla feet, his eyes mystified when his fingers clutched empty air.

I uncoiled myself. Jenny's fingers gouged even more deeply into my arm. "No trouble, Hank," she pleaded. "Please. No trouble."

I climbed to my feet, took Tony by the arm. "Let's have a drink, fella," I said.

He thought that over. His face brightened. "Tha'sh good idea," he said. "A drin'. Good idea."

I steered him to the bar. The bartender had been doing good business but looked tired. I looked at him steadily, closed one eye. "Our friend wants a nightcap," I said.

"He's had plenny," he grunted. "Too much."

"He wants one more," I said insistently. I winked again. "He needs it. Fix it the way I tell you."

He was doubtful at first. Then as he followed my directions, added a little of this and a little of that, an expression of reluctant admiration entered his eyes. Even with six different types of liquor it wasn't a long drink. But it was a shocker. It would lift the scalp off a guy who hadn't taken a drink all day. For Tony it would be more than a nightcap. It would be his lullaby.

The bartender put the glass on the table in front of Tony with an awed expression on his face. I put a dollar on the counter beside it. "Wanna lose a dollar, Tony?" I asked.

He stared at the dollar bill, rocked on his heels. "Whash ya mean?"

"I'm betting you don't knock that drink back in one gulp."

"Sure can," he said blearily. He did too. There was a wild kinda look in his eyes afterwards, but he still had enough presence of mind to pocket my dollar. I steered him across the cafe. Half way he wanted to lie down. I suggested against the wall would be more comfortable. He lay down just the same. I dragged him to the wall with his heels scraping lines through the dust of the floor, propped him against the wall, left him with his head hanging on his chest. He was breathing loudly and deeply. He didn't look like he needed anyone to keep him warm now. Even a red hot darning needle wouldn't have aroused him.

I went back to Jenny, sat down beside her.

"Thanks a lot, Hank," she said.

"Forget it."

"You sure you don't mind me being here? I feel safe between you two."

"Watch out for the guy the other side of you," I warned.

Jerry was half asleep, heard this, mumbled: "What say? What's that?"

Jenny said pacifically: "Maybe I was too touchy about that other business. But being locked in the gentlemen's toilet ..."

"You'll get your own back sometime," I grinned. "But right now you'd better get some sleep. Up early tomorrow."

"Good night, Hank," she said. "Sweet dreams."

She sure was a dame who could take it. She'd been drinking hard all evening and hadn't turned a hair. A hard wooden floor isn't the best place to sleep. But within a few minutes she was dozing, her head slipping sideways so it cushioned itself on my shoulder. I didn't object to that. Her hair was soft, her perfume used sparingly and with strategic effect. Yeah, I didn't mind it at all. I dozed off feeling happy the coldness between Jenny and myself had thawed at last.

Just after dawn, one of the cops we'd paid to tip us off rushed in with the news that Gus Morton had broken through the cordon, was heading west with every cop car in the State converging on him.

Jenny said huskily: "Thanks for the shoulder, fella." Her eyes smiled at me warmly.

"Let's talk more after we've caught up with Gus, huh?"

The way the newshounds piled out of the cafe and into their cars made it look like a hot-rod jamboree.

Me and Jerry had parked our car strategically. No one could get out the garage unless we moved first. That was fine, except for one thing. I couldn't get our car started.

I used throttle and choke, checked the gauges and wore out the battery. I still couldn't get that engine firing. The newshounds were burning to go. While I sweated and tried to get that engine firing, they surged around, pushed my car to one side so they could get going.

As each one left with a loud roar and swish of tyres against the gravel, my heart sank lower and lower. The Chief wanted an eye-witness account. And here was I, losing a big story on account of maybe a little piece of dirt in the carburettor.

Jenny was the last to leave. She stamped on her foot-brake, leaned through the driving window. "Having trouble?" she asked prettily.

I scowled at her, wiped the sweat from my forehead. "I always do this," I told her. "It gets folks worried. They think I'm in trouble."

"You'll miss everything," she said.

"Nice of you to point that out."

"Don't be a dope, Hank," she said. "There's plenty of room in my car."

Me and Jerry didn't argue. One reporter giving help to another when they're on the same assignment is unheard of. But we didn't argue. We piled in beside Jenny on the wide front seat. She let in the clutch and the car leapt forward. There was plenty of power beneath that bonnet, and it needed it. Like most women, she drove badly, and it needed a strong engine to survive her abrupt gear changes.

"Don't let the others get too far ahead," I warned.

"Don't worry," she said confidently. "I won't." Her dainty foot pressed down on the throttle. The needle climbed steadily up.

"Sporting of you to give us a lift," I said.

She smiled quietly. "You were nice to me last night."

"I always wanna be nice to you, Jenny."

Her eyes narrowed, glittered. "You weren't thinking that way when ..." She broke off, biting her lip. Then the anger melted from her face and she smiled again. "Let's forget about the past, Hank."

"Suits me," I said. "Suits me fine."

"About your car," she said thoughtfully. "Did you try connecting the leads to the plugs?"

I started at her, suspicion deep at the back of my mind. "What d'you know about it?" I demanded.

She smiled mischievously. "I disconnected them last night. Had a hunch you might want to get away in a hurry."

I roared angrily. "Why you hard-skinned, flint-eyed, brass-hearted skirt with a ..."

"That was last night, Hank," she interrupted softly, momentarily switching her eyes from the road. "That was before you were nice to me."

I stared. Then I began to chuckle. She chuckled too. "You're a good kid, Jenny," I said.

"You're not so bad, yourself, fella. Not so bad."

Gus Morton was sure giving the cops a run for their money. He drove his stolen car over the edge of a quarry pit and, while the cops were busy searching the burning wreck for his remains, took off on foot into the wooded country. By the time the cops discovered he wasn't roasting, he'd succeeded in completely losing himself.

That meant more work for the cops, another territory to be cordoned off, hours of waiting while the cops slowly closed in, attempting to draw tight an inescapable net before darkness fell.

Us newspaper folk found ourselves another cafe, slept uneasily and uncomfortably, waiting for dawn and the inevitable capture of Morton.

I awoke Jenny and Jerry about half an hour before daylight, motioned them to silence and beckoned them outside.

"The way I figure it," I said, "Morton will try to break through the cordon again. He won't do it by night. Not with all those searchlights blazing. But he'll do it just about dawn, the time when most cops will be yawning their heads off."

"You've probably got a hunch as to where he'll make the break?" sneered Jenny.

"Use your brains, Brightness," I growled. "We'll take the car now, make a continual circuit of the cordoned area. That way, wherever he makes a break, we're pretty certain to be on the spot within a matter of minutes."

"Okay," yawned Jenny. "I'm game."

Jerry said thoughtfully: "If they shoot Gus full of holes, maybe they'll put a few more in him later - just for the pictures."

It was Jenny's car, but I drove. Cops were everywhere, and the number of cop cars made it look like a bank holiday beauty spot. I drove around the cordoned area, taking twenty minutes to drive the complete circuit. I kept driving around it. The fifth time around, Jenny said: "I figure it was a bum hunch, Hank."

I scowled. "We've got nothing else to do anyway."

We were in open country now, flat grassland on either side. Jenny said suddenly: "Stop the car, Hank."

"Stop the car? Why?"

She said it with rich sarcasm: "When I was young and tender I'd have blushed, probably suffered agony because I was embarrassed. But now I'm a hardboiled newspaper woman. Why the hell d'ya think a lady wants a wolf like you to stop the car in the middle of the open country?"

I pulled into the side of the road, grinned at her cheekily. "At any rate," I said, "this is one power-room I can't lock you in."

"And don't watch!"

It was open country and, as we lit cigarettes, there was nothing to do except watch Jenny stumble across the rough ground towards a distant clump of bushes. That clump of bushes was deceptive. It looked nearer than it was. It musta been hard work for her on that rough, dew-soaked ground, with her high-heels. Yet the distant bush was the only cover. She disappeared behind it just as the shrill whine of a high-powered, hard-driven car sounded from behind us.

I turned around, glanced back along the road. A car rounded a distant bend, roared towards us like a bullet. It was a cop car, driven so furiously it swayed from side to side as the driver wrestled to keep it steady on the road. As it flashed towards us, a new sound rose on the air; the long, drawn-out wail of police sirens.

The car flashed past, almost taking the paint off my wings. I caught a momentary glimpse of the man hunched over the steering wheel, grappling with it desperately.

"Jeepers," I yelled, fumbling for the handbrake, switching on the engine.

"It's Gus," shouted Jerry excitedly. "Step on it, Hank. Get after him."

Morton had swiped a cop car, but the cops weren't far behind. Two motorcycle cops, sirens wailing madly, zoomed past me before I got the engine into top gear. I jammed my foot on the accelerator, tried to keep them in sight.

Gus Morton was trying too hard. Five miles along the road, he overturned on a bend. One motorcycle cop was too close behind to avoid him, embedded the front wheel of his bike in the back of the car. The cop went on alone for more than thirty feet. When they found him later he was badly broken up.

The other cop deliberately ran his bike up a steep earth embankment, ran the edge off its speed, jumped clear and rolled for cover behind a tree. Morton, miraculously unhurt, thrust open the door of the car, raised his head through it and cautiously looked around.

I'd arrived by this time, skidding my car broadside across the road so as not to become part of the wreckage.

The cop yelled: "All right, Morton. Climb out quietly. I've got you covered."

Morton raised his hands to show they were empty, awkwardly climbed up through the car door, jumped down the other side - the side farthest from the cop. He moved swiftly, then snaked on his belly using the car as a shield, and loosed off a couple of shots at the cop. It almost got him, made him cower back behind the tree trunk.

Jerry said excitedly: "Boy, what a chance!" He scrambled out of the car, unslinging his camera and adjusting the lens.

The copy yelled: "Hey, you two vultures. Keep out of this."

A well-placed slug sliced a chip from the tree trunk above his head, caused him to cower back again.

Jerry said with gleaming eyes: "If I can edge around the side there, I'll get a full shot of Morton behind the car, firing at the cop."

69

"You'll get a full shot," I warned. "Right in the belly."

"You wanna steal my moment of glory?" he demanded indignantly.

I watched him as he wormed his way into the undergrowth on the side of the road opposite the cop. Jerry was tubby, not meant for that kinda Indian work. What was supposed to be stealthy, silent movement sounded like the blind charging of a rogue elephant.

I couldn't see Jerry now. I couldn't see the cop and I couldn't see Morton. All I could see was the tree trunk behind which the cop sheltered and the overturned car.

Yeah, that was an idea. Using the car as a shield the same way as Morton was using it, I ran in swiftly, found myself on hands and knees the opposite side of the overturned car to Morton. I couldn't see him and he couldn't see me. There was only a few feet between us. And now I was here I didn't know what the hell I could do about it. Gus had a gun and was ready to use it. I hadn't a gun and had no authority using one anyway.

There was one thing I could do. Loose bits of metal lay in the roadway, caused by the smash. I heaved them over the top of the car, hoping they'd fall on Morton. Maybe he was panicky. Maybe he didn't know what came next. He made a break for it, let off a fusillade of shots and started running.

The cop got him, brought him down with a bullet through the knee.

He came out from behind the tree, grinning with satisfaction. I straightened up, looked over the top of the overturned car. Morton was lying some ten yards away, blood rapidly staining his trouser leg. When he fell, his gun had hit the ground and slithered ten yards away from him.

Jerry came out from concealment, face white but excited. "Got it, Hank," he yelled. "Six super-dupers. All action shots."

"What's wrong with your arm?"

He looked guilty, moving his arm uneasily. "Nothing," he said. "Just a nick. I guess Morton thought he saw a rabbit."

The other cops were late on the scene. We could only now hear their wailing sirens. We knew in their wake would be the other newshounds. I grabbed Jerry by the arm, rushed him over to the car. I got the car in movement, steered it around the wreck, edged it slowly past Morton so Jerry could take a close-up of his pain-wracked face. Then I stepped on the gas, headed towards the nearest telephone.

It was the hottest story I'd turned in for weeks, and luck was with me. An airport was close by. I drove over, Jerry handed some undeveloped films to a helicopter pilot and I did some more telephoning, arranged for a messenger to meet the helicopter when it landed in Chicago. The Chief would be doing better than he hoped. Not only an eye-witness report, but eye-witness pictures.

It was Jerry's lucky day too. The wound was just a nick. More damage was done to his suit than his flesh. He was proud of himself, sat shirtless in a chemist's shop grinning around at awed spectators while the pharmacist applied sulphide and bandages.

"I tell you what, Hank," said Jerry. "I figure we've earned a bonus."

"Better than that," I said. "Let's go back to town, put in some sleep and then paint the town a little."

"We'd better pick up our car first," he said. "Can't go back without the firm's car."

A cold hand of memory clutched at me. I gulped. "Jenny!" I said, glassy-eyed.

He gaped, eyes widening.

"Jenny," I yelled. "We forgot about Jenny!"

A guilty, hangdog expression came into his eyes. "What do you know about that?" he said huskily. "Danged if she didn't clean slip my mind."

We found her back on the road. Police cars and reporters' cars passed her continually, but all too busy to stop. She was walking bare-footed on account of she'd lost one of her heels.

Have you ever sat on the edge of a volcanic crater, feeling hot steam gushing before your face, the ground trembling beneath your feet and knowing boiling, molten rock is bubbling below you, about to spurt upwards in a tremendous surge of searing destruction?

I never have. But I know what it must feel like. Because that's the way Jenny made me feel.

Her heels were raw with walking. But that was only a minor, physical discomfort. She'd missed everything. The chase, the capture, the arrest and the midday edition. I'd made a scoop and I'd made it in her car. She naturally figured I'd ditched her deliberately, ruthlessly double-crossed her.

Me and Jerry were transformed into two hang-dog, tongue-lashed males, who shamefacedly quit her car, made our way back to Chicago without exchanging a word between us. We didn't paint the town red that night after all.

Which was just as well. Because two sleepless nights in uncomfortable billets got me sleeping through the evening and far into the night. When I finally awoke, dawn wasn't far off. I had ample time to leisurely prepare my breakfast, get dressed and arrive at the office early.

It's strange how fate works and pulls the strings which control our lives. If I hadn't arrived at the office early, I'd never have been given the Sparman assignment. And if I hadn't, maybe I'd have been a happier man, even if I wasn't a wiser one.

CHAPTER EIGHT

The Chief had his special contacts at police headquarters. When you edit a paper the size of the *Chronicle*, you need the right friends in the right places. The Chief had them. It cost plenty, but it paid off. I was at Sparman's apartment almost as soon as the police.

It was a quiet, discreet apartment block, a typical bachelor set-up: lounge, bedroom, small kitchenette and bathroom. There were a coupla cops on guard at the doorway who knew me. They didn't ask for credentials. One grinned. "Don't you guys ever sleep?"

"Tried it once," I said. "Kept dreaming of women. Couldn't stand it."

It was too early in the morning for the high-level cops to be around. The cop Captain in charge was a guy named Craig, a nice guy but not very smart. He looked worried, unsure of himself. He had a right to be worried. He had a dozen cops in there with him and all were trampling around the place destroying evidence. If there was any.

He stared at me wide-eyed. "How in hell did you get here so quick?"

"I heard a rumour," I said vaguely. I nodded towards the bedroom door. "Where's the body? In there?"

"Go take a look," he growled. "Though what the hell kick you get out of it, I can't imagine."

The cops in the bedroom were milling around, plain-clothes dicks trying to look important, falling over each other, taking flashlight photographs and picking up bits of fluff from the floor and sealing them in envelopes like they'd been sitting up all night reading Sherlock Holmes.

Sparman was as dead as a doornail. He wore a gaily-coloured dressing-gown, open and showing his sober, buff, flannel pyjamas. He was sprawled on the bed with his mouth gaping and his eyes wide like he'd never been so surprised in his life. From the waist downwards, his pyjamas became a black jelly of congealed blood. There wasn't any gun around and no guy would dream of shooting himself in that place. The inference was murder, and whoever did it stood close, coldly and deliberately squeezed off slugs, emptying the gun into the lower portion of his body.

Craig said in my ear: "A chopper would have done as good a job."

72

"Somebody sure hated his guts," I agreed.

He stared at me grimly. "You newspaper men are sure hard-boiled. How can you make a crack like that about the guy?" He suppressed a shudder. "Gives me the willies to see him lying there like that."

I looked at the dead man more closely. Although his face was contorted with surprise and agony, I had the feeling I'd seen him before somewhere. The more I gazed at him, the more certain of it I became.

"This guy's name is Sparman?" I asked.

He nodded his head. "Sam Sparman."

I crinkled my forehead. "I've seen him around some place."

"It isn't likely," he said. "He's no guy special. Works for the Regent Car Manufacturing Company. One of the fellas on the drawing board."

My mind clicked back suddenly to the reception given by the Regent Car Manufacturing Company to publicise their atomic car. Maybe it was there I'd seen him. Maybe he'd been one of the organisers.

I got it!

Sparman was the chubby, dark-haired guy with a small dark moustache, who'd displayed the sectional designs of the engine just a few moments before Marion threw her faint.

I moved closer, looked him over carefully. There was no doubt about it. I hadn't paid much attention to him then. But he was associated in my mind with Marion fainting. It's strange how the mind works. Psychologists call such things associative memory. Something important happens at the same moment something trivial occurs and you remember both incidents. You know the kinda thing I mean. You're at a speedway track and a coupla riders crash. At the same moment, the woman in front of you raises a gaily-coloured handkerchief to her mouth, lets loose a squeal of alarm. A few months later, when you've completely forgotten the incident, another dame raises her handkerchief to her mouth in the same way, and bingo, you're remembering the smash at the speedway track.

"Anything more you can tell me?" I asked Craig.

"Nothing right now. Cleaner came in this morning at the usual time, found him like this. Screamed her head off and ran into the street for the nearest cop. You can see for yourself it musta happened last night. He's ice-cold and the blood's dried solid."

"Anything known about him?"

Craig glared at me. "D'you figure we can wrap up the body, fingerprint the apartment and check all records at the same time?"

"I'll look around at headquarters later," I grinned. "Maybe you'll have something then."

"Maybe hell," he grunted. "We run the department to maintain law and order, not as an information bureau for the newspapers."

"Now, Craig," I remonstrated gently. "Newspapers can be useful to you sometimes. Especially when they remember how to spell your name."

He scowled, but in a friendly way. "Go on, beat it," he said. "Drop around later and see what we've got on file."

I found the nearest telephone kiosk, put through a call to the newsroom and dictated my report. I gave the bare facts. That was all it was possible to give at this stage. Thinking of Sparman reminded me of Doris and Marion. I'd promised to contact her as soon as I arrived back in Chicago. Well, I was back in Chicago and this was an opportunity.

I didn't telephone that I was coming. I went straight to their apartment, thumbed the bell until Doris opened up, wearing a light green, summery frock.

There were dark rings under her eyes like she'd been losing a lotta sleep, and her face was drawn. But the way her eyes lighted up when she saw me made me feel good.

She widened the door and I stepped across the threshold, removed my fedora. "How's the patient?" I asked brightly.

"Better," she said. "Much better." There was a kinda bleakness in her voice, as though she wasn't terribly thrilled by Marion's improvement.

Marion had recovered. At any rate, she was up. She was sitting on the settee, fully dressed and staring at me with large black eyes. What hit me like a blow was the floury whiteness of her face, as though her skin was made of dough. "Feeling better?" I asked brightly.

She dropped her eyes quickly to the magazine she was reading. "Much better, thank you," she said distantly. She didn't exactly slap my face with a wet codfish, but she gave me the feeling that's what had happened.

Doris said quickly, trying to bridge the unpleasantness: "Have a cup of coffee. I'm just making one."

I looked at Marion doubtfully. "If it's not any trouble ..." I began.

"Don't be silly," said Doris. "Sit down, make yourself at home."

She disappeared into the kitchen. I sat down in a chair opposite Marion. She didn't look up from the magazine, kinda shrank into herself.

"That was a nasty faint you had," I said.

"I suppose I must thank you for bringing me home," she said in a flat voice devoid of gratefulness.

"You don't have to," I growled. "I'd have done the same for a sick dog."

Stony silence.

I shuffled my feet, fumbled in my pocket, asked: "D'ya mind if I smoke?"

Stony silence.

Doris saved the situation. She swept into the room bearing coffee cups on a tray and asking me: "What have you been up to the last coupla days, Hank? You sounded terribly busy."

"Working on the Gus Morton round-up," I told her.

"Is it easy to get news stories?" she asked, pouring coffee.

"Nothing to it," I drawled. "Especially when it's crime. Sooner or later, through stool pigeons or luck, the cops get on to their man. All you've got to do is stick on the cops' tails. That way you can always get a crime story."

Marion dropped her magazine, put her hand to her forehead. Doris glanced at her anxiously. "You all right, honey?" she asked with worry in her eyes.

"I'm all right," said Marion faintly. She gave a little shudder, kinda squared her shoulders. She smiled at Doris bravely. "Don't worry," she said. "I'm okay."

"You've been getting around then?" Doris asked me.

"Yeah." I leaned forward, took the coffee cup Doris offered. "A strange thing happened today. Peculiar coincidence. A guy named Sparman got bumped off. Ever heard of him?"

Marion was staring straight in front of her like she wasn't listening to a word I was saying. Doris spooned sugar into a coffee cup, spilled a little as her hand faltered.

"He was all shot up," I said. "A chubby little guy I recognised. He's one of the employees of the Regent Car Manufacturing Company."

Doris said: "Isn't that the firm that gave the reception?" Her eyes were looking at me, wide and startled.

"That's the one. And the funny thing is, directly I saw this guy lying flat out, shot full of holes, I recognized him. He was the guy who ..."

Marion got up abruptly. "I'm going out," she said in a low but resolute voice.

Doris crossed to her quickly, took her hands, stared at her anxiously. "Are you all right, honey? You want me to go with you? Are you sure you're all right?"

Marion smiled faintly, and a silent message seemed to pass between them. "Don't worry," she said. "I'll take a walk. It may clear my head. Don't worry. I shan't be long."

When she'd gone, Doris said: "It'll take a little time for Marion to be herself. She hasn't been in the best of spirits these past few days. It's not surprising."

I said: "You were telling me what caused that shock."

"But I don't know what caused it," she said quickly. "Marion doesn't remember anything. Just remembers feeling faint and nothing more until she woke up the next morning."

"What happened in Poland?" I said quietly. "You were telling me about it. You were describing what you both went through. You were gonna tell me what caused the first shock."

"Was I?" she said uninterestedly. "Well, maybe it's better not to talk about these things now. It's all over now."

She was evasive. She wouldn't look into my eyes.

"Don't hold out on me, pal," I said. "You can't tell me half a story. The rest of my life I'd be trying to figure out how the loose ends tied up."

She shrugged her shoulders, said reluctantly: "Well, if you *really do* want to hear more about it."

I moved to the settee, patted the seat beside me. "Sit here and talk. It'll be more comfortable."

She sank down beside me, looked into the past with pained eyes. I got the strange kinda feeling that her mind was busy, figuring out what she should tell me and what she should leave out.

"Where was I?" she asked.

"You'd reached your first night in concentration camp," I said. "Sleeping three in a bunk and not getting much sleep at that."

She gave a little shudder. "It seems like a dream now," she said. "Like a horrible, revolting dream. But at the time it was all so terribly real."

CHAPTER NINE

It was the beginning that was the worst. Everything that happened was so totally unexpected and so unbearable, their minds almost cracked beneath the strain of it. Yet Marion and Doris were more fortunate than the others. They were young and healthy, had greater reserves of strength.

Slowly their soulless, routine existence began to take on a dim kind of meaning. Every day the women were roused at dawn, stumbled sleepy-eyed and shivering into the courtyard, where they lined up to answer the roll-call. They musta looked a pathetic crowd with their shaven heads, wearing only those sack-like garments. After roll-call they were split into working groups, were allowed five minutes to visit the latrine and a further ten minutes to gulp down black bread and luke-warm soup. Then each working party under the supervision of an SS guard was marched out to the field to work.

The work was back-breaking. It was potato picking, planting, ploughing, land clearance and road building. It was men's work and undertaken with the strictest supervision.

No-one could slack. Any woman who fainted was not allowed to rest but was spurred into action as soon as she found the strength to climb to her feet once more. SS guards used fists and boots with merciless disinterest.

Midday they were marched back to camp for a ten minute meal of black bread and soup and were immediately hurried back to take up their work again. Always they laboured until just before dark, whether it was winter or summer. On return to camp at the end of the day they were allowed yet another ten minutes to eat the inevitable soup and black bread before being locked up in their sleeping quarters. There they remained until the following morning when the same soul-breaking tasks were once more re-imposed.

Yeah, it was tough for them. But it was the little things that made it even tougher. The food was inadequate and they were always hungry. There were no facilities for them to wash and no means to clean out their sleeping quarters. No concessions were made to the weather conditions as far as the prisoners were concerned. Their one sack-like garment was the only clothing allowed, winter or summer. When it rained, the SS guards, warm and dry beneath their belted mackintoshes, would march them to water-logged fields where they toiled with their bare feet sinking into the mud over their ankles, the rain beating down on them, soaking their garment until its rough, wet edges chafed and rubbed their flesh raw. In winter, the women picked grass, swathed it to their feet as protection from the icy ground. There were some women like Doris and Marion who were young and able to toughen, harden and acclimatise themselves to this hard living. There were others who became weaker, fell ill and died. More died than survived. At the end of a year, nearly two-thirds of the prisoners in Doris's hut had died, so that the remaining ones had bunks to themselves.

Time can blunt most sensibilities. But not even time could dull the agonies of mind suffered by Doris and Marion. It was the unhygienic conditions they found the worst. They were never allowed to wash and still wore the same garment allocated to them when they arrived, never having an opportunity to cleanse it. The sleeping quarters were like a pig-sty. Literally like a pig-sty. It wasn't surprising. There were many women in that hut. Not all of them were able to control the normal functions of their bodies to synchronise themselves with the five-minute visit to the latrine allowed each morning. Strict supervision while they were working sometimes meant a woman would be standing in her own excrement, unable to leave her work for fear of a beating. Then there were the long winter nights securely locked in their sleeping quarters, with no way to get out and no conveniences provided.

Yet despite all this, Doris and Marion still didn't give up hope. Someone, they hoped, would be making applications, constantly pressing for their release. Somewhere, they felt convinced, United States officials were working frantically on their case, investigating it thoroughly, shifting mountains to obtain their release.

They'd been at the camp about a year when they first saw Schutz. He was the SS officer in charge of personnel. It happened this way.

Every three months the prisoners underwent a medical examination, or what passed for a medical examination. The examination concluded with the prisoners being sent to the reception hall to have their heads freshly shaved.

The medical examination on this occasion took place after they'd returned from the fields at midday. They were hustled from the dining hall, lined up outside in the hot sun. The medical officer was there, together with Schutz and two other SS officers. Usually this ceremony was supervised by the MO alone. The prisoners looked apprehensively at the three additional officers. One was short and tubby, the second hawk-nosed, with a sabre scar on his cheek, and the third was ... Schutz!

Schutz was very tall, very fair, almost good looking except for his eyes, which were a throw-back in pigmentation. His eyes were black. Coal black. And he had a brooding way of staring that made Doris feel he was able to see inside people, know what was going on in their minds.

The medical officer beckoned commandingly and a woman yoked to a large portable tank of disinfectant, bowed her frail back as she trundled it into the position the medical officer indicated. The other women watched dully. The routine was familiar to them. They could only hope they would be lucky.

The medical officer nodded to the SS guard in charge, who shouted: "Strip!"

Unemotionally, wearily, they stripped off their garment. That first time Doris had been ordered to strip, it had deeply shocked and humiliated her. But a year in the camp had hardened her to many things. The nakedness of women prisoners was commonplace to guards and prisoners alike.

Anna was the first ordered to step forward. She turned slowly, meanwhile inspected critically by the sharp eyes of the MO and the other three officers.

All the prisoners had sores. They were caused by the chafing of their rough garment, the indigestible food and the filthy conditions under which they lived. In some cases the sores ulcerated, festered and spread. Anna's pitifully thin, fleshless body possessed many scabbed sores. The medical officer glanced at her briefly, jerked his head for her to stand to one side. He did the same to the next three women. The fifth woman knew his verdict before he glanced at her. It showed in her bearing, in her apprehension. Her body was covered with festering sores, ulcerating and horrible to look at. Without a word, the MO pointed towards the disinfectant tank.

The woman whimpered. She'd undergone this experience before. She knew there was no way of avoiding it. The MO had given his instructions. She must obey.

She climbed on the wooden box provided, lowered herself until she was thigh-deep in the tank of disinfectant. She paused momentarily, fearful of what she must do next. Then, getting it over quickly, she squatted down, immersed her body until her shoulders were covered.

As she hauled herself dripping from the tank, the MO was picking out others to undergo this savage treatment. Immersion in disinfectant may be a good way to kill germs. But it very nearly killed the patients too. They danced in agony, whimpered, as, acid-like, the fluid burnt into their open wounds, seared tender membranes.

Doris was lucky. Her body was coated with dirt but, being relatively healthy, her flesh healed quickly despite the risk of infection. She had sores on her thighs where her garment chaffed but they were dry.

But as she pivoted for inspection before the casual eye of the MO, the hawk-nosed officer stepped forward, examined her more closely. She stared at him, suddenly frightened. He stepped back alongside Schutz, whispered something to him in an undertone she couldn't hear. Schutz's coal-black eyes settled on her, his head nodded emotionlessly.

Doris joined the fortunate ones who had not to undergo the ordeal of the disinfectant tank and slipped on her garment. The hawk-nosed officer watched her all the time with a strange, calculating expression in his eyes. Then it was Marion's turn, and this time it was the chunky SS officer who turned to Schutz, whispered to him in an undertone.

There was a knot of apprehension in Doris's belly. It grew as she saw Schutz's eyes rest on Marion. There was something terrible about the way Schutz stared; something brooding, horrible and terrifying in his manner.

Marion, too, was in a relatively healthy condition compared with the other prisoners. As she joined Doris, pulling her dress over her head, she whispered urgently: "Did you see that man, Doris? The one with the black eyes. He frightens me."

Doris didn't answer, because all three officers were watching Marion adjust her dress. A few moments later, when they looked away, she answered from the corner of her mouth: "Don't worry, honey. It's your imagination."

That incident should have warned them. But it didn't. When the other prisoners were lined up, marched off to the reception hall to have their stubbly heads reshaved, the guard in charge ordered Doris and Marion to stand on one side and remain at attention.

The officers drifted on to the next working group, the emaciated woman yoked to the disinfectant tank bowed her shoulders, strained agonisingly to trundle it across the rough ground. Marion and Doris remained where they were, standing in the hot sun with only a distant guard to watch them. It was the first time since they'd been at the camp that they hadn't been under strict guard.

Even so, not once did the thought of escape enter their minds. No-one ever escaped the camp. Prisoners were sometimes shot, or were electrocuted by throwing themselves on high-voltage barbed wire. But nobody ever escaped. Nobody ever thought of it seriously.

Marion said from the corner of her mouth: "We're not going to have our heads shaved?"

"I wonder why," said Doris. She raised her hand, scratched her head thoughtfully. She often scratched her head. She had plenty of reasons. During the past three months her hair had grown out, was like a boy's haircut. It had become a haven for lice.

Marion whispered with suppressed excitement: "I know what it is. Father's got things moving. We're going to be released. They daren't release us with shaved heads. That's what they were talking about. That's why we haven't gone to the reception hall with the others."

The spark of hope that was always there glowed brightly inside Doris. Marion so obviously had provided the answer. That was why the officers had personally come to inspect them, to make sure they were physically healthy. Naturally they wouldn't want to release American women prisoners when their heads were shaved to the scalp.

As they waited, they exchanged excited whispers, added one hopeful conjecture to the other until they worked themselves into a jubilant mood, feeling release was imminent, might even take place that same day. Their hopes were damped when the work party returned, freshly shaved, and they were herded back to the potato picking together with the others.

During the next few days, their hopes dwindled steadily. Apart from the one symbol of their unshaven heads they were treated no differently from other prisoners.

Then, four days later, when early morning roll-call was taken, the SS guard in charge of the working party curtly ordered Doris and Marion to stand out. The other prisoners, with startled eyes, were marched off to their labours, leaving Doris and Marion standing at attention in front of the hut. They were flushed with excitement. Exemption from the working party must have special significance. What could it mean other than imminent release?

For three hours they remained there, gazed at uninterestedly by casually passing SS guards. Then Schutz arrived, resplendent in his uniform, glistening and glittering like a new dime. He stood squarely in front of them, looked them over. It was Marion he looked at. It was as though Doris had no existence for him. The three SS guards he brought with him remained stiffly at attention, eyes looking straight before them.

Schutz said to Marion in a soft voice: "Can you guess why you haven't been sent out with the working party?"

"I think so," faltered Marion.

"Good," he snapped. He turned, gave crisp instructions to the three guards. One led the way, the other two flanked Doris and Marion.

The camp was enormous. During the time they'd been imprisoned, Doris had tried to get an idea of the number of prisoners it held. Her mind boggled at the figures. Half a million was the figure her mind wanted to reject. But all indications suggested it was even more.

It was a long walk, along new roads made with slave labour, past block after block of single-storey, brick-built villas. Instinctively they knew this was the living quarters of the SS guards and officers.

They were right. A strong door in the high wire enclosure had to be unlocked before they could enter. Then, with Schutz bringing up the rear, they were marched through neat streets of villas towards the large building which dominated all the others. It was a three-storey building with wide steps leading up to massive wooden doors. A huge swastika fluttered in the breeze above the doorway. But before they reached the foot of the steps, the guards turned off the path, went around the back of the house, followed the gravel path to the back door. It was opened by another, cheerful-faced SS guard. He and three companions had discarded their weapons, were playing cards in the back-door lobby. With his black eyes glittering with strange malevolence, Schutz motioned the two girls to enter the house, dismissed the guards who had escorted them.

Doris and Marion gaped around, a little excited and a little awed. They expected now to be escorted to an office where a legal permit for their freedom would be handed them together with their clothes.

Schutz instructed the four young SS guards in harsh tones. "You have been informed of your duties. Carry them out."

The cheerful man nodded, smiled at Doris and Marion, jerked his head to show they were to follow him. He led the way along the corridor, up the broad, thickly-carpeted stairs.

Doris hesitated momentarily before she followed him. Her heart was filled with relief as she noticed how different the attitude of these SS guards was compared with those others who rigidly enforced strict and punishing discipline upon them.

The cheery SS man led the way along a corridor, flung open a door, half-bowed from his waist as he extended his arm in a grinning invitation for them to enter. Doris and Marion were halfway into the room, the SS guards crowding in behind them, locking the door before they realised it was a bathroom.

They stared stupefied. It was a beautiful bathroom, black and white tiled, with glistening chromium-plated taps. While they stared blankly, the SS man turned on the taps, ran boiling water hissing into the tub amid a cloud of steam.

Doris asked, hardly believing their good fortune: "Do we get to have a bath?"

He grinned at her, nodded his head vigorously. "You bath now."

"And then we're to be released?"

He grinned again. "You not talk with me. We have no discussion. It is order."

Marion thrilled excitedly. "Of course we bath, Doris. How can we be released until we're thoroughly clean? We're scarecrows at the moment."

The SS man tested the water, nodded his head with satisfaction. From the rack above the bath he took down a large bottle, emptied half the contents into the water. The strong clean smell of carbolic pervaded the atmosphere. Once again he smiled, extended his arm with a slight bow from the waist, an invitation to the bath.

It was a large bath and it was quite clearly intended they should bathe together. After months of living under unbelievably filthy conditions, the hot clean water was a watery paradise.

They climbed into the bath eagerly, the SS man unable to resist jerking back his head and crinkling his nose as they passed near to him. They sank gratefully into the hot water, relaxed, allowed it to soak into their filth-caked skin. The carbolic was strong, but even after half an hour's soaking they were still by no means clean. Three times the bath was emptied and refilled before their young flesh began to glow cleanly and healthily. The SS guards had all the time in the world, sat around the large bathroom, smoking, talking and making whispered comments about the two girls.

The luxury of feeling clean and wholesome once more was so wonderful neither of the girls realised immediately the change that was taking place. A fourth time the bath was filled and, obeying the cheerful SS guard, they scrubbed their hair, scrubbed it again and again, washed and soaked it until it was soft and gleaming like black silk. Then the bath was filled for the last time, this time with sweet-smelling bath essences added so, as they soaked, the subtle sweetness of the perfume soaked into their bodies, making them smell clean, fresh and fragrant.

The SS guard nodded his approval, the two girls stepped from the bath, enveloped themselves in large bath towels handed them by other SS guards. One of the guards went out while they were drying themselves, returned a few minutes later bearing across his arm a selection of delicate, feminine underwear. Schutz returned with him, stood with his back against the door, watching Marion with his black, inscrutable eyes. She didn't notice the way he was watching her. Glowing from the bath, her skin warmly tinted, she was preoccupied with selecting from the undergarments, displayed one after the other by a grinning SS guard.

The garments were cami-knickers, all made of delicate black lace, varying only in size. It wasn't until they put them on, inspected each other critically, that they became aware of the change that had taken place.

It was the way the SS guards looked that made them realise it. They were no longer prisoners with shaved heads, filthy and half-animals. Instead they were delightfully feminine girls, fresh and glowing from a scented bath, provocative with their short hair and scanty clothing.

They both became conscious of the appraisal by masculine eyes at the same moment, became flushed and embarrassed.

Schutz was the only one not looking at them that way. There was something brooding and terrible in his black eyes as he stared steadily at Marion, stared at her so she couldn't meet his eyes. The other men noticed it, became silent and self-conscious, looked away.

That black stare of Schutz dominated the room. There was an almost audible gasp of relief when he switched his eyes from Marion, rasped stern orders.

Once again it was the cheerful SS guard who led the way from the bathroom along brightly polished corridors to another room.

It was a small room, thickly carpeted but empty except for the crude, chintz-covered armchairs and the dressing-table. With an explanatory gesture towards the dressing-table, the SS man withdrew, locked the door on them, leaving them alone.

They could have asked for nothing better. Clean, stiff brushes for their hair, hair-lotion, nail varnish, eye black, make-up and perfume. It was the complete beauty salon. They were wildly excited as they set about making themselves look attractive. Their first opportunity since they were arrested.

A little later, lunch was brought in to them on a trolley. Choice, subtle delicacies which they wolfed ravenously. Then as the afternoon wore on and they had long-since taken care of their hair-dressing and make-up, they began to worry about the delay.

Surely at any time now they would be offered clothes to choose from, taken before the Chief of the camp who would issue them their formal release.

But nothing more happened. Time passed slowly. The sun went down and they switched on the light. They hammered on the door, got no response. They became impatient and fretful, paced the floor and were almost annoyed when the next time the door opened it was another meal being served. The SS guard who brought the trolley answered their questions with a negative smile, shook his head and went out, carefully locking the door after him.

They ate. They ate because they were hungry, because the food was delicious and because they had nothing to lose by it.

"Maybe we won't be released until tomorrow," said Marion.

"Well, where will we stop tonight? Here?"

"We'll probably have a proper bed. A real bed with sheets and pillows." Marion's eyes sparkled.

There was no way of telling the time, but it was late when they heard boots in the corridor, a key rasping in the lock.

It was Schutz. Framed in the doorway behind him were four strange SS guards.

Schutz's lips smiled, but there was no humour in his black eyes as he stared steadily at Marion. She felt strange revulsion, shrank back, sheltered behind Doris.

Schutz switched his eyes to Doris, stepped close to her. His eyelids were lowered, veiling his enigmatic expression in his black eyes. He extended his hand, rested the tips of his fingers on Doris's bare shoulder. His touch was cold, unpleasant but sexless. Doris squared her shoulders, stared at him defiantly.

"It's time to go," he said.

"Where are we going?" demanded Doris.

His fingers moved quickly, hooked under the slender shoulder-strap, tugged smartly, snapping it in two. Instinctively Doris clutched the bodice of her cami-knickers as it fell, half-turned from the alert eyes of the watching storm troopers. Schutz was behind her now, fingers busy at the broken end of the shoulder-strap, tugging it, snapping it away from the garment.

His sudden change of attitude was shocking and surprising. Doris stared at him with angry eyes, outraged almost to the point of smacking his face. Then, as his black eyes stared into hers, the menace of them reminded her of their position. They were still prisoners in a concentration camp, surrounded by uniformed SS guards. They were abject slaves compelled to do the bidding of their masters, and any show of defiance would be met with vicious brutality. Without taking his eyes from Doris, Schutz barked an order across his shoulder, and one of the SS guards stepped forward. Over his arm was a black georgette negligee which he held out, held ready for Doris to wear.

Suddenly the fear was back inside her, knotting in her belly so her knees wanted to tremble. Schutz's eyes were glaring, red-rimmed and commanding. She obeyed his unspoken command, allowed the SS guard to hold the negligee while she slipped her arms into it. It meant the unsupported side of her bodice fell clear, exposing her bare breast. But that no longer seemed to her to matter.

It was Schutz himself who tied the girdle while she stood numbed, arms hanging limply at her sides. He tied it tightly so it emphasised the curve of her hips, left it gaping at the front to show the lacy under-garment against the whiteness of her thighs.

She was in a haze now, heart pounding loudly, ugly fear knotting inside her with the realisation she had been wrong all the time.

Her head began to clear as two of the guards hustled her from the room. She heard a wail of protest from Marion, but the door slammed behind her, cutting it off. Then Schutz was leading the way and she was following, every step she took revealing the smooth softness of her thighs as they broke through the parted negligee.

Schutz stopped before one of the doors in the well-lighted corridor, knuckled the panels. A harsh voice answered, and Schutz opened the door, gestured to Doris she must enter. When she hesitated, the two guards behind urged her forward roughly, thrust her into the room, closed the door behind her.

It was a bedroom. She'd known it would be that instinctively. As she stared around her like a startled animal looking for some means of escape, the hawk-nosed officer who had whispered about her on the parade ground, moved leisurely towards her. She backed away from him with wide, scared eyes. He smiled, produced from the pocket of his dressing-gown the key of the door and deliberately locked it.

"Do you speak German?" he asked.

She glanced with a shudder at the large, double bed with counterpane folded down ready for use, and nodded a tongue-tied assent.

He was completely at ease, almost amused. Placed ready for use, was a small round table with champagne glasses and a magnum of champagne in an icebox. Slowly, almost leisurely, he poured two glasses, refitted another cigarette to his long holder, lit up and then brought a glass across to where Doris stood trembling in the middle of the room.

"You are shy, my dear," he said as he handed her the glass. At the same time he was eyeing her appreciatively, his eyes frankly lustful, concentrating on her unsupported bodice. She used her hand protectively, and he tut-tutted.

"Come, my dear. You can't be that shy. And it's so hot in here. You must take off your negligee."

A kinda numbness overcame her so she was cold and lifeless. She stood like a statue while he untied her girdle, drew the negligee from her shoulders and threw it to one side. But when he tried to embrace her, she slipped away from him, put the champagne table between them.

86

He laughed heartily as though she amused him immensely, sprawled in a chair, emptied his glass of champagne at a gulp and poured more. He motioned to a chair, said pleasantly: "You might as well sit down. You don't get much opportunity in the camp, I imagine."

She perched herself on the edge of the chair, stared at him with a hard, set face, while his eyes fingered her body. She'd felt naked before, but never so naked as at this moment.

"You're an American," he said conversationally.

"That's right," she admitted tonelessly. Her flesh ran cold as his eyes fingered it.

"You should drink the champagne," he said. He narrowed his eyes slightly. "You'll probably need it."

"I've made up my mind," she said firmly. "I won't agree. I want to go back to the work camp. I won't agree to this."

He smiled tolerantly. "You will," he said confidently. "You'll agree. And the champagne will make it easier."

"I don't want any champagne," she said dully. She banged her glass on the table, watched with narrowed eyes as he shrugged his shoulders, poured himself a third glass.

"You'll be sorry about the champagne," he said sadly.

She pressed her lips together, didn't answer.

"How difficult you are being," he commented. He held his long cigarette holder gracefully, blew a fine plume of smoke towards the ceiling. "Will this be your first time?"

She suppressed the shudder that ran through her, clenched her hands tightly and said nothing. He stared at her solemnly for several minutes, puffed gracefully at his cigarette the whole time and poured himself yet another glass of champagne. That emptied the bottle.

A little later he leaned forward, reached across the table towards her. She wrenched away from him, and for the first time he showed anger, sprang to his feet, kicked his chair away. "I have tried to be friendly and pleasant," he said angrily. "Am I to have it thrown in my face?"

"It is not my wish to be here," she said quietly.

"Get up," he roared.

She hesitated, then slowly climbed to her feet.

"Stand to attention," he rasped.

She was still a prisoner receiving orders. She stood to attention, knees together, hands flat against her sides. He stared at her, walked slowly around her, staring until the flush spread from her cheeks to her neck.

"Are you going to be friendly, little one?" he asked in a low, menacing voice.

"I won't give way to you," she said quietly but firmly.

"Very well," he rasped. He strode across the room to a writing bureau, opened a drawer and took out a long dog-whip.

He brought it back to Doris, displayed it before her eyes, showed her the smoothness of the plaited leather, hard and unyielding at the haft but tapering to a sharp, flesh-cutting tip.

"You understand this?" he asked, moulding and flexing it between his fingers. "It can cut, sear and kill." His voice was harsh and metallic, his face flushed. "Do you want your flesh to become torn and bloodied, skin stripped until it's hanging in shreds?"

She felt faint, closed her eyes and swayed slightly.

"Do you?" he roared.

She opened her eyes, stared into his, was numbed by the mercilessness she saw glaring out at her. She moistened her dry lips, unable to speak.

"Perhaps you do not believe," he rasped. "Perhaps you do not understand what can happen. I will show you."

He walked to the nearest armchair, picked up a silken cushion. He poised himself, threw the cushion in the air and, as it fell, slashed viciously.

There was strength in his arm, powerful, cutting strength. The vicious hiss of the lash was drowned by the sharp thwack of leather biting into the cushion.

Doris stared with wide, horrified eyes as the cushion fell, stuffing spilling on the floor.

There was a wildness in his eyes and perspiration on his forehead. He towered over her, held the whip beneath her nose. "Well, what is it to be?" he demanded thickly.

She didn't answer. She couldn't. The knot of fear in her belly was choking her. Her mind wanted to shout she wouldn't do it, but her body was still flinching from the impact of the dog-whip, knowing next time it would be her own flesh and blood splitting and spilling out beneath its cutting agony.

"You do not learn easily," he growled. He backed a coupla paces, allowed the whip to trail on the floor, poised his arm for action. "It is wiser and less painful to decide before than after," he pointed out.

She stared at him pitifully, her lips trembling.

His eyes were gleaming viciously. "Where will you have it?" he asked brutally, pointing. "There or there!"

Her eyes filled with tears, her lips trembled pathetically. She saw the ruthlessness in his eyes, the strength in his arm, and his hawk-nose resembled that of a vulture about to shred her flesh. The sound of the splitting cushion was ringing in her ears and she knew the cutting lash would descend again and again.

He moved his arm tentatively, and suddenly the tension inside her broke. Blinded by tears, she stumbled towards the bed, sobbing as she slid her slim legs down between the sheets.

Hawk-nose tossed the dog-whip to one side, chuckled as he shrugged off his dressing gown and turned out the light.

* * *

Breakfast was served in bed. Doris was worn, listless and burnt out. She didn't even want to eat.

Hawk-nose himself had completely lost interest in her, ate his breakfast ravenously, ignored her as he dressed, went out leaving her lying in bed. As soon as he'd gone, she climbed out of bed, ran to the door. It was unlocked, but the SS guard outside seized the door handle, slammed it shut again.

Nothing could alter what had happened. That it was a commonplace occurrence was clearly shown by the methodical way Doris and Marion had been carefully groomed. But how long did it go on?

This humiliation was far worse than any other she'd suffered in the camp. The experience itself was revolting. But far worse was the knowledge her actions were dominated by fear, that even her emotions and temperaments could be gauged goaded to false but pleasure-giving intensity by the threat of the lash.

She was shamed, humiliated, broken in spirit and body. She paced the room, crying and praying she would not experience this man again and again.

When the door opened next it was Schutz. He eyed her expressionlessly. "Strip," he ordered curtly.

She had no existence independent of her captors. Her bodily actions were governed by them, decided upon by them and demanded by them. And now she'd undergone the final humiliating lesson of learning her mind and emotions too could be moulded and controlled by them. She stripped as ordered, felt the eyes of the SS guards curiously examining her naked body as she was herded along corridors, through well-lighted offices where uniformed clerks, men and women, glanced at her indifferently, and out through the wide front doors.

Marion was already there, waiting between two guards, her youthful body looking fresh and clean in the sun but her dark eyes underlined with black rings.

The two girls looked at each other wordlessly. Both knew what the other knew. Both were broken, mentally and physically. Doris saw the angry blue weal that curled around Marion's thigh and felt again a surge of impotence at their inability to resist these monsters. While they lived they had no choice. Theirs was but to obey and suffer.

Four guards marched them across the camp to the reception hall. It was not busy at this time. They waited, watched each other being shaved to the scalp without a trace of feeling. Once again they endured the torment of the disinfectant, ran with stinging flesh through the laughs of SS guards to the shelter of the issue-hut where they were issued with the familiar sack-like garment.

They had a moment to talk. Doris whispered: "Was it dreadful?"

Marion said in a flat voice: "I can't bear to talk about it. Don't mention it again."

"It was the little fat man?"

"Yes," said Marion dully. Her eyes stared in front of her. "I'm scared, Doris," she confessed. "I'm scared all the way through. What if anything should happen? What if ..."

"You don't have to worry," said Doris comfortingly. "Nothing will happen. That was the beginning and the end of it. Nothing ever will happen because you have to love a guy before ..."

An SS guard yelled at them to hurry. Pulling the sack-garments over their heads, they hurried across the yard towards their sleeping quarters. It wasn't their lucky day. The working party had just finished lunch. Doris and Marion were caught up with them, marched off to potato picking through the long hours until sunset.

But terrible as their conditions were, they would have preferred them to what happened later.

And what happened later was ... Schutz!

CHAPTER TEN

Doris broke off abruptly as a key sounded in the door of the flat. "We mustn't talk about it in front of Marion," she whispered quickly.

"About the shock," I urged. "How did she get the shock?"

"Some other time," she whispered, then raised her voice and added loudly: "... so after that I never accepted any of her invitations to go to her party." She glanced around at Marion, smiled warmly. "How are you feeling now, honey?"

"Better thanks," said Marion. She didn't look better. Her face was chalk-white and there were dark rings beneath her eyes. She walked straight past me like I didn't exist, into her bedroom. She slammed the door loudly behind her. No dame could have said more clearly she didn't want me around the joint.

I got up, reached for my fedora. "I'll see you around sometime," I told Doris.

She didn't press me to stay. "That's right, Hank," she said. "Come around again." She nodded her head towards the bedroom. "She's still not well. And it takes a long while for her to thaw and get sociable with folks."

"I'll be around," I said.

I lunched at the Press Club, went on to the office afterwards. There was a message on my desk. The Chief wanted to see me. When I entered his office, he was chewing a cigar savagely, glaring red-eyed at the lunch-time edition lying on the desk in front of him.

"Something on your mind?" I asked.

"Yeah," he growled. "This guy Sparman." He made a rude gesture with his hand. "What kinda news story d'you call that?"

"You've got the facts," I told him.

"Facts!" he sneered. "Who's got what facts? Who is Sparman? What did they find out about him? Where did he come from? Who shot him? And why?"

"Look, Chief," I defended. "I was there almost as soon as the cops. They hadn't a thing on him. You don't have to worry. I'll drop by headquarters later and they'll give me everything they've dug up."

His blue eyes glared, he rifled through the mass of papers on his desk, came up with a sheet torn from a scratch-pad. "So you're gonna get the dope from the cops, huh?" he said sarcastically.

"They've got their finger on things," I said defensively. "They keep records."

"Sure," he growled. "When it's straightforward. They've been working on it a coupla hours now. D'you know what they've got?"

I shook my head. "Could be anything."

"I'll tell you what they've got," he said with malicious satisfaction. "Practically nothing. All they've been able to find out is what his employers told them." He referred to the memo sheet. "Joseph Sparman, employed for four years by the Regent Car Manufacturing Company. Has no relatives, no next-of-kin. Their records, based on information Sparman gave, show he was in the Army, wounded and invalided out. Wounded in left leg. Sparman produced no references and, because of man-power shortage at the time, was employed on the strength of engineering designs he drew and submitted. That's all they've got on him. No friends, no relatives, no enemies. None of his property's been stolen and there's no hint as to why he was shot. Much less who did it."

His steely eyes were fixed on me. The Chief has a kinda sixth sense. He knows when a news story's worthwhile going after. He figured this was worth following up.

"Okay," I growled. "So the cops have got a coupla hours start on me. You want me to turn up all the stuff they can't find out. Is that it?"

"They're not bothering with it, Hank," he said, less sharply. "Headquarters have got plenty on their plate. My contact there just told me it's gonna be turned over to routine investigation. They figure this can wait. It'll be followed up through the normal channels, each angle followed through slowly. It'll take time, Hank. It'll take months. You know how the cops work when they make a routine case outta anything."

"You want I should work on it all the time?"

He leaned forward across the desk. "Get your teeth into it, Hank. See what you can find out. It's strange a guy having no friends or relatives. Maybe he's switched his name, got a past. Get your teeth into it for a coupla days. If you don't get anywhere then, drop it. But it's worth a try."

"Any suggestions where I should start?"

"Yeah," he said. "Start at the bottom. Work your way through. Put your finger on those things the cops haven't noticed. The cops go for the obvious. You oughta try the not so obvious."

"What if I don't get anywhere?"

"I'm not expecting miracles. Just have a slap at it."

I shrugged my shoulders, pushed my fedora to the back of my head with my forefinger and lit a cigarette. "Tell me one thing," I said. "If you had a gun and wanted to kill a guy, would you empty six slugs low down in his belly?"

"I'd give him one straight through the head," said the Chief.

"Okay. Give me a theory on that."

He leaned back in his chair, rolled his cigar from one side of his mouth to the other. "Viciousness," he said. "The guy who shot him knew he wouldn't die immediately. He was probably a hop-head, enjoyed every moment of Sparman's agony, shot him with cold-blooded mercilessness."

"That as good as solves it," I jeered sarcastically. "All I do now is go and look for a hop-head. There can't be more than twenty thousand in Chicago."

He glared at me. "G'wan, beat it," he growled. But the twinkle in his eyes belied his voice.

"I'll be seeing you," I grinned.

The Chief said to start at the bottom. I did. When a guy's been knocked off, use him as the starting point.

It's strange the way a dead guy seems different in the morgue. Back there in his bedroom, dressed in his pyjamas and sprawled back across the bed with a grimace of agony on his face, Sparman had been a man. A dead man for sure. But just the same, you knew he was a man.

Down there in the cold morgue it was different. When they pulled back the white sheet he was like a white wax model. The doctors had been to work prying out the bullets. He wasn't a pretty sight. Slugs had done a lotta damage and surgical knives had added to it. I was used to seeing stiffs but this one gave me the willies. I hadn't before seen a guy with the lower part of his body completely shot away.

I looked him over. It didn't get me anywhere. I looked him over again. The morgue attendant pulled at the sheet, began to pull it up his stiff legs.

"Justa minute," I said. I examined Sparman more closely. I hated it but I had to do it. I grasped his left leg, lifted, examined it close up.

"Don't worry," sneered the attendant. "He ain't got fleas."

I let the leg go and it thumped back on the marble with a noise like wet meat. I lit a cigarette with a shaking hand, went out thoughtfully. The Chief had said: *"Look for something the cops have missed."* I'd found something the cops had missed. Sparman had a war record, had been invalided out of the Army because of a slug through his leg.

But there wasn't a mark on his leg, not even the slightest scar where he could have been nicked with a bullet.

* * *

In these days when the man in the street is pushed around by Government officials from the day he is born until the day he dies, you meet up a lot with red tape. Red tape is like red rag to me. It gets me fuming, hot under the collar so I wanna blow my top.

That's what made it tough for me wading knee-deep in red tape. I ran up against more red tape than I'd ever met before in my life. The hell of it was, I had to hold my temper in check, try to keep down the simmering anger which constantly threatened to boil over.

It was Army red tape I got swathed in - the worst sort. I only wanted a simple thing; a glance at the records of one Joseph Sparman, one-time soldier.

I filled up dozens of forms, obtained letters of authority from important folk, nearly went crazy trying to convince bland-faced, white-collared guys behind clean desks I was a *bona fide* journalist. Finally I got half what I wanted.

They gave me the information grudgingly like it cost them a hundred bucks a word, and there wasn't much of it at that. It confirmed what I already knew. Sparman had no living relatives, was invalided out from the Army with a bullet in the leg that fractured the bone. But there were other items which contradicted facts I already knew. The Army records showed Sparman as being nearly six feet tall. The murdered man didn't come within three inches of that height. The record card showed Sparman had undergone three operations on his leg, a piece of bone removed and replaced with silver plate. An operation like that would have left a surgical scar inches long.

I was sweating by the time I'd learned this much. I worked hard not to let the bland-faced clerk realise it.

Sparman the murdered man was not Sparman the soldier. First I'd have to prove they were not one and the same man, then somehow I'd have to find out what happened to Sparman the soldier.

The Army clerk could tell me nothing useful. Sparman had worked on his own account, had lived in hotels before he volunteered for the army. If he'd deliberately set out to give no information about himself, he couldn't have succeeded better.

I said hopelessly: "Well, if that's the best you can do, I get just nowhere."

His bland face smiled like he got real pleasure out of not being helpful. He closed Sparman's file, put it in the out-going tray. "Sorry I can't do more," he said with satisfaction.

"If only there was something to get my teeth in," I mused. "Just a little something, any kind of lead."

"Sorry," he smiled.

I shrugged my shoulders, turned towards the door.

Maybe it was his off-day. Or maybe his cold official heart was somehow touched by the dejected slope of my shoulders. "Just a minute," he said quietly.

I turned around. He was frowning, his face serious like he was scolding himself. "I shouldn't be doing this really," he pointed out.

"You got something," I said eagerly.

With an infuriating slowness, he reached to the out-tray, retrieved Sparman's file, placed it neatly on the desk in front of him and opened it slowly. At the back of the file was an envelope, opened and addressed to Sparman. He cleared his throat, coughed a coupla times, flushed slightly and said: "You will treat this as confidential?"

"Sure," I said. "It's between you and me."

"This letter was received by the Army authorities after he left the service. We couldn't forward it to him. We didn't know his address."

"I'd like to see it," I said.

He held it between his fingers. "A slight irregularity," he said. "This letter was opened in order to be returned to the sender. The letter got mislaid. It was never returned. I guess it's too late now to send it back. All that was four years ago."

"Just let me look at it," I said. "If it'll only give me a lead ..."

He still held the envelope, still looked thoughtful. "You know," he said, "it's embarrassing having this letter in the file. Nothing must be destroyed, of course.

"Yet if that letter were noticed it would cause awkward questions." He looked at me meaningfully and thoughtfully. "You'll excuse me for a few minutes?" he asked. He placed the letter on the desk within easy reach of my fingers, got up and walked to the door. He turned with his hand on the door-knob, treated me once more to that bland smile.

"I'll say goodbye in case you're not here when I get back," he said smoothly. He closed the door very quietly behind him.

That letter might have been an embarrassment to him. It wasn't to me. I don't know how long he was away or where he went. But I do know that when he came back, I wasn't there. Neither was the letter!

I could see where his embarrassment came in. The writer was a dame who called herself Rose Slack. Weeding out the endearments, the pleadings and the veiled threats, it added up to a few simple facts. Rose was gonna have a baby, Sparman's baby. Rose wasn't married to him. She wanted him to get in touch with her, marry her before her condition became obvious.

95

That letter had been written four years earlier. No wonder the Army clerk figured it was a little late to return it to the sender and advise her to get in touch with Sparman through some other medium.

A lot can happen in four years. But I did manage to find neighbours who remembered Rose Slack. Rose and her mother moved out of the district some four years earlier. I figured I knew the reason for them moving.

Then I got a hot lead. One of the neighbours had seen Rose serving behind a counter in a fashionable store.

My feet were growing as flat as a cop's. I was snuffling cold trails as no cop ever did. Rose didn't work at the fashionable store any more. No, she'd left when she got married. I even squeezed something out of that, got the guy Rose married. That led me south to a Chicago suburb.

It was afternoon and it was hot. I travelled all the way by taxi, asked the driver to wait. As I walked up the path of a neat little suburban villa, I was beginning to wish I'd never seen that letter.

I had to knock and ring several times before the door opened. She was a homely little thing with bright eyes and a wide, generous mouth.

"Mrs Robins?" I asked politely.

She stared at me with puckered brow, as though trying to remember where she'd seen me before. "That's right," she said, with a questioning note in her voice.

"I'd like to have a few words quietly with you, if I may."

Her eyes became mildly startled. "I'm afraid I don't know you. What is it about?" She jerked her head around, called along the passage towards a sudden thumping noise. "Jimmy, stop that noise at once. I gave you the hammer to play with, not break the house down."

She turned back to me with a warm smile, inviting my co-operation in the scolding of her son. "You know how children are!"

"Yeah," I said. "He'd be about three, wouldn't he?"

Her eyes narrowed. "Who are you?"

"Don't get worried," I reassured her. "There's just one thing I wanna know. Where can I find Sparman? That's all there is to it."

A kinda veil came down over her eyes. "I don't know what you're talking about," she said quickly. Too quickly.

I jerked with my thumb. "That's Sparman's kid banging holes in the floorboards."

She went white. "How dare you," she said. "That's my husband's child. You can't blackmail me. I'll call the police."

"Rosie," I said quietly, disarmingly. "I don't want to harm you. I just want five minutes' talk. Afterwards you'll never see me again, never hear from me."

96

Her eyes showed she was trying hard to believe me. She backed, held the door open. "Come in, just for a minute," she said. I saw her hands trembling.

We were standing in the hall now. She was toying nervously with the hem of her apron, no longer worried that Jimmy was pounding the floorboards hard enough to break the hammer. He looked pretty much like other kids of his age; spiky hair, dirty face, crawling on hands and knees.

"I deny everything," she said, panting. "There's not a word of truth in anything you say."

I held up my hands to quieten her flow of denials. "I just wanna know one thing," I said. "D'you know where Sparman is now?"

"I don't know anything," she said. Her lips set in an obstinate line. "I don't know what you're talking about."

I thought that over. I surely needed co-operation, but I couldn't look at her when I made the threat. "Maybe I should come back and talk it over with your husband?"

I heard her sharp intake of breath followed by a long pause. "I did know a man named Sparman," she admitted grudgingly. Her voice was a whisper.

I still didn't look at her. "Four years ago you tried to get in touch with him, wanted him to give a name to your child. That child!"

"Do you want to crucify me?" she wailed. "There's the kid too. D'you wanna crucify him? Sparman wasn't the only fish in the sea. What if I did marry another guy? Neither you nor anyone else can prove Jimmy isn't my husband's child."

"I'm not trying to prove that," I said slowly. This time I did look at her. I tried to make my eyes tell her I was speaking the truth. "All I want is news about Sparman. You knew him. You must know some way I can contact him."

She stared at me levelly. "That's really all you want?"

"That's all I want, Rosie," I said sincerely. She was a nice kid, was settled down with a husband. Why should I wanna bust that up?

She said slowly: "I saw Sparman once. It was a coupla years ago. It was just after I was married. Just before Jimmy was born." Her face hardened. "It gave me a turn seeing him. Getting out of a big new car he was. Had a blonde with him. A peroxided blonde." Her eyes flashed with sudden hatred.

"D'you know where I can contact either of them?"

There was a long pause. She drew a deep breath, said slowly: "Look, mister. Sparman doesn't mean anything to me any longer. I want you to know how it is. But right then while I was having Jimmy, it kinda knocked me over. Even though I was married, I still had a yen for that guy. I followed them." Her lips curled. "She was a floozie. A high-class floozie. He went home with her like they were old friends. I guessed what she was right away. Asking around confirmed what I thought." Her voice broke. "It kinda breaks you up being thrown over for a tart."

"Do you remember the address?"

"Aw, I don't know. It's such a long time ago. I've forgotten it all now."

"Think about it," I urged. "I've gotta find Sparman. Think about it, will ya?"

She thought about it. She remembered the street, but didn't remember the number. She remembered the house, and its approximate position, described it for me. She didn't know the blonde's full name but knew everyone called her Susie.

"Thanks for the information," I said. "I hope you and your husband make a real go of it."

Her eyes narrowed inquisitively. "Just why are you wanting Sparman ...?"

Little Jimmy banged once too often, didn't get his fingers out of the way in time. He set up a howl that lifted the ceiling. She rushed to him like he was trapped in a flaming building. I opened the front door, closed it quietly behind me and was probably half way back to town before she noticed I'd left.

Susie lived in a middle-class district and wasn't difficult to find. The first guy I asked grinned at me wickedly. "A blonde named Susie? Lives around here? Sure I know her, fella. Who doesn't?" He winked. "She'll give you a good time."

My ears were red. "I'm just not sure which house," I mumbled.

"That one there," he pointed. "You don't knock. Up on the second floor." He leered. "If she ain't expecting you, better make sure she ain't got no visitors."

I found my way to the second floor. The typewritten slip on her door said: "Susie Bell." I knuckled the door three times before she opened up. She looked like she hadn't been long out of bed and was halfway towards putting on her warpaint for the evening. Her cheeks were white and her lips colourless, but her eyelashes were long and spiky, thickly black.

"What do *you* want?" she rasped, automatically resting one hand on her curving hip.

"You," I said.

She opened up and I stepped inside. It was a large room, clean but untidy. The bed was dishevelled, ashtrays full of butts, unwashed glasses scattered around, and used coffee cups on the table.

"I don't know you," she grated resentfully. Her voice was harsh and metallic, high-pitched like a file scraping over corrugated iron.

"Mind if I sit down?" I relaxed into the nearest armchair, pulled a cigarette case from my pocket, lit up. She lounged across, stood looking down at me with her hand still on her hip.

"I don't know you," she repeated.

"We'll get acquainted."

"Who sent you," she demanded, her voice raised an aggressive half-pitch.

"Sparman sent me," I said. "He gave me your address."

Her brow puckered, her eyes brooding. "I don't know any guy named Sparman," she snarled. "What do you want?"

"What does a guy usually want with a dame like you?"

"I don't have fellas barging in without an appointment," she flared. "I've got a right to a little privacy, ain't I?"

"So Sparman told me."

Again her forehead puckered. "Sparman? Who is this guy?"

"You ought to remember. Used to be a friend of yours."

"I ain't got no friend of that name."

"Three or four years ago," I said. "A tall guy, dark; he's been in the Army. Got a blighty in the leg. Owns a big car. You know him all right. He's been up here with you."

Her eyes widened. She stared at me like I was crazy. "You mean Joe Sparman?"

"Sure. Who else?"

Her eyes narrowed. "What are you giving me?" she demanded bitterly. "What fool trick you trying to pull?"

"Nothing to it," I drawled. "Just a question of me being lonely. Sparman gave me your address, told me where to find you."

Something was wrong. The way she was staring at me, the incredulity in her eyes, showed it. But at the same time, her brain was working like lightning, weighing up the situation, trying to reason it out.

"Just what do you want?" she demanded bluntly.

"It's like this," I said. "I kinda lost touch with Joe. I figured maybe you could tell me where I can find him."

She played for time, dropped her eyes, reached out, took the cigarette from my hand and puffed at it slowly. Her eyes wouldn't meet mine and I guessed why. She knew something and was figuring how much she could make out of it.

"Just how long since you saw Joe Sparman?" she asked casually; a little too casually. She still wouldn't look at me.

I thought that over quickly, plunged desperately. "A coupla months."

She turned away from me, swayed to the window with her hand caressing her hip, emphasising the way it rolled. "Just how bad d'you want to know where to find Joe Sparman?" she asked without turning her head.

"Pretty bad."

"How much is it worth?"

She was a gold digger. Whatever I said, she'd dig for more. "Ten bucks," I told her.

She snorted derisively. "Enough for a subway ticket. I live well, fella!"

I switched on a disgusted tone. "Twenty bucks and that's the limit."

"Go chase a kite," she drawled over her shoulder.

I got up, mumbled clearly so that she could hear. "A guy wants to contact a buddy and he's bled white. That's the way life is, I suppose." I walked to the door, began to open up. It was bluff. I didn't really intend leaving. But it worked.

She turned away from the window. "Okay," she drawled. "I'll take the money first."

I shut the door again, reluctantly fumbled in my pocket, produced twenty dollar bills. She took the dough with the air of a queen accepting a bouquet, tucked it out of sight in her bodice. She was smiling now, her eyes contemptuous. "Just how long ago did you see Joe?"

"Coupla months," I grunted.

She twisted her lips mockingly "I don't know what you want, fella. But you can't do Joe any harm now. You didn't see Joe two months ago. Because nobody's seen him for years."

I stared at her.

"He was a good guy, that Joe Sparman," she said. "Too bad he killed himself."

"Killed himself?"

"That's what I said," she snarled. "He's dead. D'you understand? He's dead. He's where you or nobody else can get at him."

"I didn't know," I faltered. "I thought ..."

"I don't care what you thought," she snarled with surprising vehemence. "Now leave me alone, will ya? I just don't want you around." Surprisingly there were tears shining at the back of her eyes.

"I didn't know," I said again. "Was it ...? I mean how did it ...?"

"The car," she said. "The damaged car he was so proud of. He went over to Falcon Heights one night. There was a road subsidence and he always drove fast. Smashed clean through the guard rail. Nobody could get near till the car burnt out."

I said: "Can you tell me anything about him? Any friends or relatives he had where he lived; can you tell me anything?"

Her eyes were in the past, misty and remembering. "I don't know," she said dully. "I'd known him such a short time. I knew so little about him." There was a kinda break in her voice. She was fighting hard to hold back tears, and suddenly she wasn't a floozie any longer but a dame remembering a guy she'd loved, and it was hurting, torturing her.

"Get out," she choked. "Get outta here, will ya."

There was just a chance she might remember something. I took a visiting card from my wallet, propped it against an empty gin glass. "If you remember anything, it'll mean dough in your pocket," I said.

Her shoulders were shaking, there was a suppressed sob in her throat when she said flatly: "Get out. Get outta here."

I got out. I went downstairs thoughtfully to the waiting cab.

Back at the office, I thumbed through yellowing newspaper records for the account of Sparman's accident. We didn't have enough to go upon, so I pulled strings, obtained permission to inspect the Registrar's records after office hours.

I learned a whole lot of things then. But none that meant anything. Sparman had died right enough in that car. When his charred body had been retrieved from the wreck, all that remained to identify him was the metal Army tag around his neck. No relatives or friends turned up to identify the body at the morgue. The verdict of the coroner's court was accidental death.

I'd followed a long cold trail, had reached a dead end. There was just one thing I knew the cops didn't know.

Inexplicably, when Sparman died, someone went on living in his name. That same man had been murdered.

I'd come to a dead end following all the leads to Sparman the soldier. Now I'd start all over again, this time following the trail of Sparman the murdered man.

CHAPTER ELEVEN

Sparman's employers weren't helpful. In fact they were the opposite, resentful not only of the routine police questioning they'd undergone, but also the taint of being connected in any way with a murder.

The manager refused to see me, capitulated when I sent back a thinly-veiled threat that business firms should always co-operate with the press if they wanted the press to co-operate with them. He gave me as little information as he could.

I wouldn't have relied on him anyway. If you wanna know about a guy, you don't ask his employers. You ask the folk who work with him, the fellas he drinks a beer with at lunchtime, the pretty girl who takes down his letters in shorthand.

When I emerged from the manager's office, I acted like I had all the authority in the world, stalked over to the nearest desk and asked a neat-looking, bespectacled clerk to show me the office where Mr Sparman used to work.

I acted like I'd bought shares in the company. He behaved like he thought I musta bought most of them. He scuttled in front of me, anxious and fawning, along corridors and past offices until we reached the department labelled: "Structural designing."

There were glass windows all round that set of offices. I asked the clerk to point out the desk where Sparman worked. I noted the guys working nearby, memorised them. Then, with a brief thanks, I sent the little clerk scurrying back to his desk, found my way downstairs into the street.

I was waiting outside a coupla hours later when the staff came out to lunch. I spotted one of Sparman's work buddies, jostled him as he was crossing the road. "Remember me?" I grinned.

He stared. He had a cheeky face with a turned-up nose. "Can't say I do."

"I'm a friend of Sparman."

He said "Oh," and his mouth dropped. The tips of his ears turned red. "You're a cop then?"

I let it ride. "Let me buy you a beer," I suggested.

He looked nervous. "Well ... I ..."

"I insist," I said, smiling genially.

He took it as an order from a cop. "Well," he sighed. "If you insist ...!"

I bought him a double Scotch. He thawed under the warming influence of it. His name was Flaxman, and he'd worked in the same office as Sparman for the past two years.

"Not exactly a sociable kinda guy," he said. "Kept himself to himself, never went out evenings with anyone from the office."

"No close friends?"

"The guy's dead," he said, meaning you don't knock a dead guy.

"He was murdered," I pointed out.

"Okay," he growled. "So nobody liked him. But there wasn't any reason special for that. There was something unpleasant, unnatural about him. He had black eyes and a way of staring that made you think of slimy things."

For some strange reason, when he said that, it reminded me of Doris, the way she'd described Shutz's eyes staring at Marion.

I excused myself from Flaxman, tried to date Doris for lunch. She'd had lunch but had time to spare later, would meet me for a stroll.

When I got back to the bar, Flaxman was toying with an empty glass. I re-ordered, questioned him some more about Sparman.

"He was a queer cuss," he admitted. "Never talked about himself, never seemed interested in anything except work. Used to stay late night after night, working all hours, poring over all the designs. Made it bad for me and the other fellas."

"But he must have had hangouts," I said. "If a guy lives in Chicago, he has to be seen around somewhere, even if its just a hash joint."

His eyes crinkled. "Wait a minute!" he said. "Now I do remember something. A coupla years ago it was. We had a rush job, all stayed late that night. We went out to dinner, came back afterwards and worked on. There were four of us. We argued about the best place to eat. Sparman said he knew a place that wasn't too bad. It's such a long while ago I don't remember it clearly but, Sparman seemed to be known there."

"Think," I urged. "See if you can remember where it was. The name of it."

"I'm not sure," he said doubtfully. "I think if I was to drive around, I might recognise it. It was such a long time and ..."

I had him by the arm, was propelling him towards the door. "Hey, wait a minute," he gasped. "Where are we going?"

I signalled a taxi, bundled him into it as it drew into the kerb. "You start in remembering," I rasped. "Just keep driving around. I wanna find that restaurant."

Flaxman gave instructions to the driver. After driving around a time, Flaxman told me nervously: "It's somewhere around here.

I know it's in this district somewhere." He sat forward, giving more instructions to the driver, growing red in the face as he sweated. It didn't seem like he was getting any place. There were plenty of restaurants in that district; one we passed three times, newly painted and as conspicuous as a May-pole. The fourth time we passed it, Flaxman rumpled his hair feverishly. "It's somewhere around here," he said desperately. "A foreign kinda place, if I remember."

"The only foreign place I've seen is the *Grunwald*."

He sat up straight, eyes shining. "That's it!" he said. "What you said. Say it again."

"The *Grunwald*."

"That's the name of it," he said with assurance.

I told the driver to turn around, drive back. We stopped outside the newly-painted restaurant. Right on top where you wouldn't normally notice it was the name "Der Grunwald".

Flaxman looked at it, doubtful once again. "I don't think this is the joint."

"It's German."

"Doesn't feel right," he doubted. "I didn't think ..."

"It's been freshly painted," I pointed out. "May have looked different then. Let's take a gander inside."

Up the steps, through swing doors and into a broad restaurant. Flaxman looked around with awe. "Well, what d'ya know?"

"This it?"

"Sure is," he said. "Looks different from the outside, but this is the joint right enough."

I dug down in my trouser pocket, pulled out a ten dollar bill. "Settle the taxi, will ya, Flaxman? Thanks for your time." I gave him my visiting card. "Anything else you remember, give me a ring. It may be worth your while."

He looked at my card, he looked at me. "Gee," he said. "Are you a reporter?"

"Right now I'm a foot-sore nosey-parker. Now be a good fella, will you? Scram."

He pushed off, clutching the ten dollar bill in his hand and walking like he was in a dream. He'd spent his life sitting at a desk, calculating figures and drawing geometrical designs that would drive me crazy in a coupla minutes. Yet half an hour of being with me doing my kinda job had got him burned out. He was half-dazed after being caught up in a sudden eddy of newspaper activity and being dropped abruptly.

I chose a table waited on by a short, thick-necked, hard-headed, German-looking guy. He draped an off-white napkin over his arm, rolled up to my table and showed me his sweating face. My guess was right. He handed me a menu and asked: "Vot vos it, heh?"

104

"I wanna learn something about a friend of mine," I said. "A guy who used to eat here regularly. A guy named Sparman."

He had deep grooves in his fat cheeks that ran from his nostrils to the corners of his mouth. Those grooves lengthened and deepened. "Sshparman!" he whispered in a hoarse voice.

I had him and I knew it. He knew Sparman and probably knew he'd been murdered. Had read it in the papers, maybe. All I had to do was keep him on the hook. I put my hand in my pocket, slid out my wallet and opened it. I spread it on the table where he could see it, bulging with dollar bills.

The mention of Sparman's name may have scared him. But the wallet held him there as though magnetised.

"I can pay for information," I said softly.

"But Sshparman," he said in a breathless voice. "I joost know dis man von name. Vot for he come every night? I know heem. Sure I know heem. But vith heem I nefer talk. I know heem not."

He glanced over his shoulder as the manager came out of the office. I picked up the menu, glanced through it. It was German food: every conceivable type of sausage with sauerkraut. "Don't you know anything about him?"

"I know nutting," he said. "I nefer speak except take orders. He nefer speak vith me."

"Looks like you're not gonna earn today," I said.

He gazed lovingly at my open wallet. "I know nutting," he repeated almost tearfully.

"But you must know something," I insisted. "Surely he wasn't always alone. Sometimes he must have had friends with him."

He shrugged his shoulders with a man-of-the-world meaning. "Vell, of course, every man has friends. Judy was with him many times but den, of course ..."

"Judy?"

He nodded. "Joost a dame," he said deprecatingly.

"If Judy knew Sparman, I wanna know Judy," I said.

"You not know Judy?" he asked incredulously. "You not know Judy Miland? Die blonde vot vorks in ze nightclub ofer ze road."

I peeled him a ten dollar bill from my wad. "Give," I said. "Give all you know."

He didn't know much but it was enough. Judy Miland worked in the nightclub across the road. She frequented the restaurant from time to time, and some six months earlier had met Sparman. A kinda friendship had developed between them. Quite often they were in the restaurant together. That was all he could tell me.

The nightclub was shut fast. It didn't open until twelve at night. Prolonged hammering on the door got a response from the caretaker. He didn't know Judy's address, but a ten dollar bill jolted his memory so I could look for her address under Judy Buck in the telephone book.

I didn't forget my appointment with Doris. The chances were Judy was still in bed anyway. I caught a taxi, met Doris in the park, and we strolled together beneath the shade of the trees, sat on the rustic seats overlooking the goldfish pool.

"Marion's much better today," she told me. "I'm hoping she'll be fit enough to take a holiday."

"Good idea," I said. "Where are you thinking of going?"

"Florida," she said. "Follow the sun is a good motto."

"Listen," I said. "There's one thing I still haven't got clear. This shock Marion experienced in Poland. How did it happen? And what actually caused it?"

She looked at me solemnly. "Honestly, Hank," she said sincerely, "I haven't the faintest idea what caused it."

"But you were gonna tell me," I pressed her. "You were gonna tell me how it came about and ..."

"I can only tell you what I know, Hank."

"You were telling me," I said. "You'd been introduced to a dog-whip."

"You want I should tell you more, Hank?"

"Sure," I rasped. "I hate it. Hate every moment of listening. But I've gotta know more. It's all so unbelievable, yet I've just gotta hear about everything."

"Schutz was the real cause of the trouble," she said.

"Yeah," I said. "I remember Schutz. A tall, fair guy, with a moustache and black eyes."

"It was Schutz who was responsible for Marion's shock," she said dully. "Because from then onwards, he seemed to haunt us."

That animal-like existence she'd suffered in the camp still lived realistically in her mind. So much so, she'd hardly begun to talk before I was transported to that camp in Poland, found myself among the weary, bowed, half-clothed women as they worked or were herded into their sleeping quarters.

They saw Schutz again about a week after their visit to the officers' living quarters. By that time, through contact with other women and through living in the same hut, they were as verminous and as filthy as ever.

Schutz appeared at lunch roll-call, stood at a distance, staring at Marion until her lips twitched and her knees began to tremble. He stood watching, his eyes boring into her as the work party was herded away to the labour fields. Doris stumbled along beside Marion. "That man Schutz," she whispered. "Did you see him staring at you?"

Marion scratched vigorously at her head, which wore a stubble like a man's two-day beard. "He frightens me," she confessed. "It's the way he looks."

"Try not to let him see you," advised Doris. "Keep behind the others when he's around."

But it was not so easy. Schutz arrived at odd times, always stood at a discreet distance during roll-call, watched Marion all the time. But that was all he ever did. And so she became used to it. Marion would stare back at him, return stare for stare, but never entirely succeeding in ridding herself of the feeling of revulsion induced in her by his eyes.

The hard, monotonous work continued day after day. Roughened, work-grimed fingers bled from scrabbling in the loose earth, back and shoulders ached intolerably from continual stooping, the pain of strained muscles through long hours of standing was almost unbearable, and always there was the hard bite of hunger through insufficient food. But as the weeks passed, the grim fear of pregnancy that had lodged inside them disappeared, and they were almost content to endure their labours now that other and greater fear had been demolished.

Conditions in their sleeping quarters became worse due to the influx of many new prisoners. They were sleeping two in a bunk now, using blankets that had been filthy and verminous when they'd arrived at the camp eighteen months earlier. The hut was worse than a pig-sty. Even sties are cleaned out occasionally. The newcomers had coughs and brought with them a new kind of disease which rapidly spread, starting with acute irritation followed by inflammation and finally turning into an ulcerating rash. The irritation was so intense none could resist scratching. Then, when the skin was broken, germs infested the tissues.

When the medical officer made his next quarterly visit, not one of the prisoners was free from the running sores and ulcers.

Misery that day was acute. Not one prisoner escaped the tank. All had to undergo the baptism in disinfectant, including Doris and Marion. Then, limping with the sting of it, stumbling and huddling their burning, sore-infested bodies, they were herded still dripping to the reception hall for head-shaving. All of them except Marion, that is. Because Schutz had been present at the medical examination, had whispered to the medical officer, who instructed Marion to stand on one side after her baptism.

Doris could barely wait to have her head cropped and get back to Marion. She needn't have worried. Marion was sill standing at attention as ordered, went out with the work party, conspicuous with her boy's crop among the other bald heads.

Marion whispered to Doris when she got the opportunity. "I won't go through it again. I'll kill myself."

Doris said comfortingly: "Maybe there's another reason for it. You don't have to always expect the worst."

"I'll kill myself," said Marion simply. "I'll do it somehow. I'll kill myself."

Doris kept a close eye on her after that. Days passed and became weeks. The weeks passed slowly. No guards called for Marion to escort her to the officers' quarters. But there was always Schutz. Every three of four days, arriving at roll-call, standing and watching Marion with those black, inscrutable eyes.

Another three months passed, and again it was the medical officer's tour of inspection. Schutz was there, stonily watching Marion as the file of stripped women presented themselves before the eagle eye of the medical officer.

The previous immersion in disinfectant had served some purpose. Only a few prisoners were deemed necessary by the medical officer to undergo immersion.

Once again Schutz murmured something to the medical officer, who looked at Marion, nodded his head, motioned her to one side. The rest of the prisoners were marshalled ready to be marched to the head-shaving.

It was then Marion broke all the rules of the camp. She stepped up to the medical officer, head held high and eyes defiant. "I wish to have my hair cropped like the others," she demanded.

The MO stared at her. It was a blatant defiance of discipline and moreover had taken place in front of the other prisoners. It was the kind of situation in which a prisoner might have to be publicly punished, lashed into unconsciousness before the eyes of her fellow workers.

But Schutz saved the situation, moved in quickly, inserted himself between the MO and Marion.

"You are to change your work," he rasped. "You are to become office staff, officer personnel working under my supervision. Office staff are allowed to wear long hair."

Marion stared at him. Stories had filtered through to her of the lucky prisoners allowed to work in the offices. They handled the records, slept in a dormitory, were allowed to wash and even wear civilian clothes. It was unbelievable good fortune. But the fear of Schutz was strong inside her. She burst out, a little wildly: "I want my friend to go. I can't go without her. We must keep together."

Schutz's face hardened. For a moment it seemed as though he would strike her. Somehow he held himself in check, the corner of his mouth quirked as he turned to the MO, spoke to him, nodding towards Doris. In turn, the MO spoke to Doris. Neither of them were sent for hair-cropping. Instead they were told to hold themselves in readiness for transfer.

It seemed like a lucky break, yet several more weeks elapsed before they heard any more. Then one cold morning when the summer weather was beginning to break and the work party was shivering at early-morning roll-call, Doris and Marion were told to drop out.

The transfer was like being whisked up from hell and set down in paradise. In such a large camp, keeping official check of prisoners as they arrived, were discharged or died was a big undertaking.

The records office was a long, two-storey building, lined with filing cabinets and record-card indexes. It was situated within the wired-off section of the camp allocated to the SS guards.

Doris's fears and apprehension as they were marched once again into that wired-off enclosure were quickly dispersed when they were escorted by guards to the records office, left alone there to adapt themselves.

The records office was in itself a prison. But so clean, so unbelievably different from what they'd been though, it didn't seem like a prison.

Twenty girls worked in the records office, each having a desk and a set routine task. Their living quarters were upstairs on the first floor. They were cramped because, with Doris and Marion, there were twenty-two of them in a small dormitory. But each girl had a bunk, cleaning tackle was available, and a connecting bathroom, equipped with hot and cold water, provided them with the luxury of being ever-clean, as well as the facility of washing sheets and clothing.

Yeah, clothing was available too. There was a trunkful of it in the dormitory. Prisoners used the trunk as a kinda pool, switching and changing clothes with each other and deriving a small pleasure from being differently dressed each day. Doris and Marion were too pleased at the opportunity of wearing clean and pretty clothes to ask questions. But both knew where the clothes came from. The came from the hot and sweating bodies of incoming prisoners who would later be issued with a sackcloth garment to replace these.

There was one other luxury. A tiny kitchen had been provided. Food was rationed to them each day and was in short supply. But it was much more than Doris and Marion had received while working in the fields and, as they were able to cook for themselves, the food could be made appetising.

At the end of a week, Doris and Marion had settled down to a new and almost pleasurable routine. In the morning, the door of their dormitory was unlocked and they had a whole hour to wash, dress and prepare their breakfast. When the bell rang, they went down to the office, sat at their desks and proceeded with their work under the steady gaze of an SS officer, who sat at a large desk, in a commanding position.

Their work was simple. Doris, for example, copied out a duplicate of the record card of every incoming prisoner. Marion's task was equally simple. She had to transfer the details of each record card to one large-sized summary sheet. Forty record cards could be entered on one sheet, and each sheet was locked into a leather-bound ledger.

They worked steadily through the morning, not allowed to talk, and if their eyes lifted away from their work, a warning grunt would come from the supervising SS officer.

At lunchtime they had two whole wonderful hours to prepare food, eat and rest. Then back to their desks where they worked until the day's quota of record cards had been documented to the final stage of filing. A further two hours was then allowed them to cook their evening meal, and finally they were locked in their dormitory until the morning should begin the routine again.

It didn't take Doris long to understand the situation. All the girls in the records office were specially privileged. They were all young and attractive and could allow their hair to grow until it reached their shoulders. SS guards, whose sleeping quarters were in the very next building, strolled into the records office during the breaks, talked freely with the girls.

There was no roll-call when the dormitory door was locked, and every night, three or four girls would be missing. From their barred dormitory windows, Doris and Marion could see the guards' sleeping quarters, the moving shadows on the blinds, hear the blare of a radiogram and the high-pitched shrieks of girlish laughter.

Marion told Doris: "I mean it. I won't go through it again. I'll kill myself some way. I can't do what these other girls are doing."

It was as though the other girls understood their resentment. Doris and Marion were isolated, not spoken to by the other girls, who joked about their experiences together while they looked at Doris and Marion mockingly.

But the weeks passed without any pressure being brought to bear on Marion and Doris. They could almost have been pleasant weeks except for Schutz. There was always Schutz!

Schutz was in control of the records office. He had an uncomfortable knack of entering at odd times, leaning against the wall smoking, and all the time his black eyes fixed on Marion. It was as though she was a candle and he was a moth. He just couldn't keep away from her, couldn't stop watching her. But what he felt for Marion was hard to guess. His face was hard, his eyes brooding but sexless. He was not interested in women as women; Doris knew that instinctively. There was something strange about him, something that wasn't normal.

On the last day of the month, they learned, there was to be a dance. It was part of the official routine. The SS guards who were bachelors were entitled to entertainment. Therefore those prisoners who worked in the records office, because they were the most presentable of prisoners, were to perform the duty of dance-hostesses. It wasn't a request. It was an order.

The girls were wildly excited, talked about it for days ahead. The SS guards were excited too, went to a great deal of trouble to prepare their sleeping quarters for dancing, decorated it, laid in a stack of sandwiches and drinks.

Three days before the dance, Doris learned how the girls obtained their pretty dresses. She was one of six girls escorted from the records office to the underground store where hundreds of thousands of familiar brown, manila envelopes were stored.

They were escorted there by SS guards and were supposed to be checking the filing of the envelopes. But it was a facade. The other girls, who had quite obviously been there before, eagerly ripped open the more recent envelopes, plundered them, discarded everything except the most expensive dresses and underclothing. Meanwhile, the guards rifled through the smaller manila envelopes, pocketed the more expensive of the jewellery they found.

As they were marched back to the records office, each girl bearing an armful of clothing, cheeks flushed with excitement, Doris was thinking of the women who had originally worn them, women now verminous and filthy, labouring in the fields, shovelling rubble or yoked to heavy, two-wheeled carts, straining with weak, emaciated bodies to shift a ponderous weight.

For the next few nights, an extra hour was allowed the girls before retiring. The bathroom was in constant use as the girls soaked, washed and dried their new clothing. From somewhere, one of the girls managed to obtain an iron. Finally, when the new clothing was ready to wear, the clothing they'd used for the past month was carried to the garbage heap where, in due course, shaven-headed, skeleton-like prisoners yoked to hand-carts loaded and dragged it away to the incinerators.

On the actual day of the dance, one of the SS guards brought them a supply of make-up. Even though Doris and Marion were apprehensive, they could not resist the rush of excitement which thrilled the other girls, and they themselves dressed at their best, made themselves as presentable as possible, getting pleasure from doing so.

The dance was nothing like as bad as they had feared ... at first! The floor had been cleared, flowers festooned the room,

111

the radiogram was a beautifully-made job and the SS guards were clean, smart, exceedingly charming and polite.

Both Doris and Marion were resentful and unsociable, not speaking unless spoken to and replying only in monosyllables. The other girls entered gaily into the spirit of the affair, talked animatedly, danced willingly, with sparkling eyes and flushed cheeks, drank too much champagne and ate lots of sandwiches.

It was difficult for Doris and Marion to be unsociable. Those keen young men, with their soft grey eyes, polished manners and courteous thoughtfulness, were attractive and charming. It was difficult to meet their engaging smile with a blank stare, to remain hard and unbending when they were so pleasant, so obviously wanting to be friendly.

But neither Doris nor Marion could eliminate from their minds mental pictures of other and similar young men, wearing the same uniform and with the same soft grey eyes, who would screech through the night in heavy cars and ransack houses and take innocent men and women to the jails. Such men smashed prisoners to their knees with rifle-butts, mercilessly shot down men and women, old and young alike, all in the name of a creed they worshipped fanatically and were willing to die for as well as kill.

Schutz was there, sitting in a dark corner, unobtrusive and brooding, his black eyes all the time watching Marion so she was willing, anxious to have partners to dance with. Yet as she danced, intermingled with the other couples on the floor, answered in a dull voice the questions of her partner, hardened her shoulder muscles to his gentle, insinuating and almost pleasurable pressure of fingers between her shoulders, never for one moment was she free from Schutz's brooding, black-eyed scrutiny that was frightening in its intensity.

Later the tone of the dance began to change. The SS guards were drinking schnapps. There were bottles of it, and they drank it like water. The girls were drinking champagne, much more than was good for them. The party became wilder as the men became boisterous. One of the girls lost her blouse and thought it was a huge joke. Wearing a blouse became out of fashion. With the eager help of the men, all blouses were discarded.

Marion and Doris retired rapidly to a corner, where they watched what ensued with wide, anxious eyes. Doris had seen what was coming, had twisted away quickly from her partner. Marion hadn't been quite so lucky. Buttons were ripped from her blouse and the guard who had done it was still swaying in the centre of the room, blearing around as though trying to find her.

Although he looked in Marion's direction, he was too drunk to see her, reeled across to the nearest table, swallowed another glass of schnapps at a gulp and sprawled in the nearest chair. There were more guards than girls. It was fortunate for Doris and Marion that so many of the guards were too stupefied by drink to circulate. As it was, the number of girls able to stay on their feet exceeded the number of men. That was fortunate for Doris and Marion because they were able to sit quietly in a corner without being bothered.

Without anyone bothering except Schutz, that is. He sat and stared, stared until Marion's knees trembled and she wanted to cry.

The girls had spent a lotta time cleaning and ironing their undergarments and prettying themselves. They were in a champagne mood, proud of their sex and proud of their bodies. The dancing became wild and abandoned, a sensuous rhythm of music inducing in the too closely-clasped couples the mood to fondle one another.

Doris and Marion were stone-cold sober. They watched with revulsion as the couples danced, the girls moving their bodies provocatively, giggling hysterically as eager hands gripped them.

It was no longer a dance, it had become a debauch. Necking was indulged in with brutal openness, most of the girls in their underclothing and not much in it at that. One girl with a drink-stupefied smile on her pretty face, danced a solo while the others clapped their hands in time, chanted the rhythm. She musta had dancing experience at some time. She had good rhythm, good movement, and a good body. There was nothing to restrict the abandonment of her dancing. She wore only her stockings.

It was sickening and unbearable to watch. So sickening that even under the eyes of Schutz, Doris tried to leave. That move had been anticipated. The door was locked. All they could do then was shut their ears and eyes to what went on. That wasn't so easy, because the lights were blazing down and drink had eliminated all self-consciousness. Bared guards and girls behaved like they were alone in the privacy of their bedrooms. And while the radiogram blared interminably, swaying couples drifted towards the far end of the room where the guards' bunks had been pushed to make space for the dancing.

There seemed no end to it, the lights on, the radiogram playing perpetually. Some couples drifted off into sleep, but as they did so, others sobered up, recommended dancing and continued the debauchery.

Throughout it all, Doris and Marion sat white-faced, erect and sleepless, watching the grey light of dawn slowly flood into the room and living only for the time when they would be herded back to the sanctuary of the records office where they could launch themselves into work and forget this scene.

Sleepless and untiring all the time, Schutz, inscrutable and unblinking, sat staring at Marion.

But an end comes to all things. Sleepy, woolly-headed, the girls were ushered back to the records office in time to wash, eat breakfast and be ready at their desks when the bell rang.

Doris and Marion had been lucky. Their unwillingness to take part had gone unnoticed and no real unpleasantness had been forced upon them.

But their luck lasted exactly two days. It was broken by Schutz. It was always Schutz, always around, always watching Marion.

He appeared a few minutes before the end of the working day, lounged carelessly against the wall, his fair hair slick and greased so it glistened whitely in stark contrast to the velvet blackness of his eyes, which he levelled at Marion.

As work finished and the girls rose from their desks, he paced slowly across to Marion, stood squarely in front of her. "You will come with me," he instructed.

He saw the fear in her eyes, sensed the trembling of her knees, noticed the quick, despairing look she cast at Doris as though seeking help. His eyes flicked to Doris. "You come too," he ordered, and turned on his heel, strode towards the door.

There was no question of disobeying. They followed him apprehensively, at the same time wondering if perhaps at long last they were to receive news of their release. They followed him to his private office, the small villa where he worked and slept.

When they entered, there were three SS guards lounging at neat desks, laughing and smoking. When Schutz entered, they hastily scrambled to attention. A curt order from Schutz put them at their ease. As they relaxed, their eyes switched to Doris and Marion, scrutinised them with dull disinterest.

Schutz paced to the far end of the room, unlocked a stout door with a key he carried in a pocket beneath his tunic. He beckoned. "Come here," he ordered curtly. "No, not you. Just that one." His finger was pointing at Marion.

Marion approached him timidly. Doris remained where she was, standing at attention with the three SS guards watching her, indifferent.

As Marion got level with Schutz, he pointed into the room. She stepped across the threshold, drew back quickly. Schutz gave her a violent thrust between the shoulders, followed after her, locked the door behind him.

Instinctively, Doris started after them. The disinterested attitude left the three guards. They moved quickly and easily, intercepted her. "Stand at attention," growled one.

"I want my friend," wailed Doris desperately. "I want to go with my friend." She tried to push past them.

One guard jutted his lantern jaw in her face, grinned cheerfully, and backhanded her viciously, knocking her to the floor. She thrust herself into a sitting position, half-dazed by his savage blow, saw him grinning down at her as though it was all very friendly and playful.

"On your feet and stand to attention," he grinned.

She didn't move quickly enough. They helped, dragging her up on her feet by her hair and arms.

Lantern-jaw said grinningly: "Stand to attention. Do as you're told. Stand to attention and don't move a muscle. D'you understand?"

Doris nodded dumbly, too dazed by the blow to worry much about Marion.

"Hands at your side," grinned Lantern-jaw. "That's it. Fingers fully extended. Now hold your hand up. Draw your belly in. Square your shoulders. That's right. When I say attention, I mean attention."

It was a strained, unnatural position. The guards sat between her and the door where Schutz and taken Marion. They joked, smoked, played cards. The minutes ticked past slowly, and Doris began to wilt through standing in that strained position so long. She was worried, too, about Marion, scared what was happening to her.

Lantern-jaw threw down his cards with a rueful grin, lounged to his feet. One of the others began to deal a new hand as he walked slowly towards Doris and with unsuspected speed and violence drove his fist deep into the pit of her belly. As she rolled on the floor, doubled up in pain, sucking agonised breaths into tortured lungs, he grinned down at her. "Keep your belly in," he ordered. "Stand to attention when you're told."

His boot goaded her ribs. Blinded with tears and panting with pain, she clambered weakly to her feet.

"Stand here, beside me," he directed. She stood at the side of him, breasts heaving, breathing rasping in her throat. He took a ruler from a desk, placed it on the table beside him. "Extend your right arm," he instructed. "That's it. Now keep it that way."

The other two guards chuckled like it was a huge joke. Doris stood with her arm extended at right angles from her body. There was nothing to it at first. Then as the guards continued their interminable game of cards, her arm became heavier and heavier. Her shoulder muscles began to ache with the strain of holding her arm that way. Her arm was growing numb, bloodless and unfeeling. It was turning to lead. She bit her lip, shut her eyes and concentrated on holding her arm horizontally. It became beyond human endurance.

115

Lantern-jaw picked up the ruler, casually slashed her across the knuckles. "Keep that arm up," he rapped.

The arm was no longer numb. The sharp burning agony of cracked knuckles brought life back into it. She whimpered, tried to hold her arm steady. Her hand trembled, her lips trembled. She concentrated, felt the sweat beading her forehead, and the game went on interminably.

The third time the ruler cracked across her knuckles, she fainted. When she recovered consciousness, she was lying on the floor with her skirt around her waist. They were watching her, grinning expectantly. She moved, winced, and discovered the revolting trick they'd played on her. They roared with laughter as she hurled the ruler at them blindly, shuddering with loathing.

They left her alone after that, allowed her to lie on the floor while they played, growling at her to keep still whenever she moved.

Two hours musta passed before Schutz's door opened and he emerged, stripped to the waist, glistening with sweat. "Get food," he ordered. Then, when he saw Doris staring at him with wide, frightened eyes, added: "Get her out of here."

Doris didn't go easily. They gripped her painfully in an ungentlemanly way, dragged her, protesting and crying, back to the records office. On the way, they passed one of the many heavily-laden hand-carts which were always to be seen, drawn by prisoners.

This one was slewed halfway across the path and was almost beyond the strength of the woman drawing it. Lantern-jaw left Doris in the grip of his companion, snarled at the prisoner: "Get to the side of the road."

The woman was completely naked, as were nearly all those who drew such wagons. The rope yoke which fitted across the shoulders, frayed and wore away their solitary garment, and it was not always possible for prisoners to obtain a new issue. This prisoner was a tall skeleton, arms and legs as thin as broom-sticks. Her ribs were starkly revealed, almost splitting through the skin, and her breasts - the only fleshy part of her body - through continual stooping as she strained against the ropes, had sagged heavily, become flat and elongated like two thick folds of flesh drooping almost to the waist. Her body was covered with ulcerating sores, and as she strained to obey Lantern-jaw's command, the yoke-ropes cut deep into the grooves they'd already made in her bare shoulders, cut deep into wounds that were continually bleeding, never healing.

The woman was bent almost double with the effort she was making. Bone joints stood out in stark relief, with skin stretched transparently across them, the misshapen breasts swung loosely

116

as she arched with exertion and the hand-cart slowly, very slowly, began to move.

It didn't move quickly enough for Lantern-jaw. "Too slow, too slow," he roared, and his upraised fist pounded the pitiful, shaven and defenceless skull. The woman sprawled on her face, lay without a whimper. Then, at his terse command, she weakly struggled up on to hands and knees. Her physical condition was appalling. It was obvious that even with the best of medical attention, good food and rest, her chances of survival were small. If she continued this terrible labour she would die soon, very soon.

Lantern-jaw knew it, accepted it as commonplace. There were many deaths in the camp every day. If there hadn't been, there would have been insufficient room for all the prisoners. He jeered at Doris. "See this specimen? How would you like to take her place when she dies? She will die very soon now."

He and his companion chuckled as though it was a great joke. Wearily the bowed woman raised her face to stare at him. Her face was a death-mask, skin strained taut over cheekbones and jaws so the outline of the teeth showed. But her black eyes were suddenly alive, glowing as though she now knew hope. And the hope she embraced had been contained in Lantern-jaw's comment. She would die soon.

Doris stared at the pitiful figure, and when she recognised her she almost fainted with the pain of pity. For the woman was Anna; Anna the exquisitely-dressed girl with the umbrella who had been so concerned about her hair. And here she was, not two years later, turned into an unrecognisable skeleton, flesh rotting on the bones while she lived.

Doris no longer needed urging. Only too willingly she hurried away from Anna, hurried towards the records office. The memory of Anna was eating into her mind. She remembered Anna's crime which had brought her to this place. With signs, a few words of German and much concentration, Anna had told Doris how she spent a fortnight's holiday in England, had corresponded with an English girl. She hadn't been given a trial, had been visited by the police, who after questioning had escorted her to the camp.

Doris was locked in the dormitory for the night with the other girls. She was tortured alternately by memories of Anna and concern for Marion. She was sleepless all night, and the next day Marion still didn't return. It was the third day Doris got her opportunity. She slipped out of the office undetected, made her way hurriedly towards Schutz's villa. She burst in, without knocking, rushed to the locked door uselessly before Lantern-jaw and his two companions could get to her. They dragged her from the door, hit her brutally. She screamed Marion's name again and again, and they smothered her mouth to stop her screams. In the midst of it the door was unlocked, Schutz himself stood in the doorway staring out at them. He was stripped to the waist, perspiring and with a two-day stubble of beard on his face. His black eyes glowed angrily. "I told you to send that woman away," he rasped, and slammed the door.

Doris had committed a flagrant breach of discipline. Under camp discipline she would have been flogged almost to death. But for obvious reasons, Doris wasn't officially punished. In Schutz's own villa, the guards imposed their own punishment, and used their belts on her bared haunches, afterwards dragging her, semi-conscious and bleeding, to the records office and up to the dormitory, where she was handcuffed to her bunk by wrists and ankles. She lay there for many days, semi-delirious with pain, nursed and fed by the other girls, who were contemptuous of her stupidity.

Eight days later she was released, was allowed to continue with her work. She went downstairs and half-sat, gritting her teeth with pain as she tried to catch up with her work. She'd learnt her lesson. Defiance earned her nothing except grief. She could only hope Marion would return soon, that nothing terrible had happened to her.

Marion did return. Four days later, escorted by two SS guards. She'd been stripped, and the angry bruises on her arms, legs and body were ugly and clear to see.

But it was only Marion's body that returned. Her mind had gone. Her black eyes, set wide and expressionless in her white face, stared unseeingly in front of her. Doris got up from her desk, rushed over to her. The two SS guards turned away, with their lips curling contemptuously. The other girls stared wide-eyed and frightened as Doris tenderly took Marion by the arm, led her upstairs to the dormitory.

Marion's mind had shrunk to the proportions of a baby's. If an order was shouted loudly enough she would obey it, numbly and dumbly. Otherwise, she seemed to hear nor see nobody, was unconscious of her surroundings. If she was put in a chair, she would remain seated for hour after hour, unmoving, black eyes staring into nowhere. She could neither dress herself nor wash, feed herself or even control the simple functions of her body.

At first, Doris nearly went crazy. She pleaded for a doctor, insisted on a doctor and was beaten for her insolence. And for some strange reason Marion was allowed to remain in the records office. This meant Doris could look after her, nurse her, feed her, give her all the care and attention a mother gives a baby. While she was working at her desk, Marion would be sitting or lying on her bunk, staring into nowhere with unseeing eyes.

It continued month after month until Doris feared Marion's brain had been completely destroyed. Then slowly, a little at a time, Marion began to improve. It took a long time, a very long time. She wasn't even properly recovered when, much later, they were finally released from the camp by the liberating armies.

Doris saw Schutz only a few times after Marion was returned. His visits were purely official and concerned with the work of the records office. He never even glanced at Doris and had apparently completely forgotten the existence of Marion. A few months later, changes were made in the administration, Schutz was transferred, and discipline was tightened up all round. It meant there was more supervision in the records office, longer hours of work, the cessation of social relations between the girls and the SS guards, and strict incarceration.

Discipline was likewise tightened up throughout the rest of the camp. As the long months passed and became years, it became increasingly apparent to Doris that neither she nor Marion would have survived had it not been for that strange whim of Schutz's to transfer them to the records office. That transfer had been almost fatal for Marion. But it had saved Doris's life. And this she always remembered, always felt she owed everything to Marion, whose mental suffering had been the price to pay for both their lives.

There was a strange dryness in my throat when I asked: "What was it Schutz did? What could a guy do to drive a dame crazy?"

Her eyes narrowed, hardened with suppressed hatred. "I don't know," she said.

"What d'you mean, you don't know? Surely you asked Marion? She'd have told *you*."

Her eyes turned to mine, the misery of remembrance causing them to overflow with tears. "She was so sick, so ill. It was months before she was even able to remember her name. And then, when she was almost well, I did ask her what happened. I only asked her once!"

"What did she say?"

Doris shook her head. "I'd never ask her again," she breathed. "It musta been something terrible, horrible. When I asked her, she stared at me for a moment and then fainted straight off. Went out like a light. She was unconscious twenty-four hours. Since then, I've never dared ask, never will again."

"The poor kid," I said. "The poor kid!"

She got up, smoothed her dress with her hands. "Don't ever mention it to her," she warned.

"I won't," I said. "I won't. But there is one thing I'd like to do."

"What's that?"

"Get my hands on Schutz," I gritted. "Tear him in pieces."

CHAPTER TWELVE

She called shortly after I arrived at the office the next morning. Our freckled-faced office boy told me with a broad leer that Miss Bell was waiting to see me.

I wasn't surprised he leered. Her perfume was a thick cloud that engulfed me at ten yards, her short skirt was tight enough to split, and was split deliberately at the hem, so it showed her legs almost to her stocking-top. She wore a winning smile, a ton of cosmetics, a purple wisp of a hat with a tail feather, and a wide-necked blouse. She musta been reading some gay-nineties fashion notes, adapted her brassiere to lift herself high, threatening to spill out through the over-wide neckline.

"Oh, Mr Janson," she cooed in her harsh voice, and extended her hand to me, holding it high and arched, like she'd got the idea from the same book.

"Hiya," I said, and cleared my throat. I looked around uneasily. The boys in the newsroom were suddenly amazingly active, passing in and out through the swing door of the reception room, giving Susie the eye.

"I wanted to talk to you."

"About what?"

"About Sparman," she said.

Jim Flukes, who had passed through a moment before, came back, stared at Susie's blouse like he wanted to nose-dive, pushed through the swing doors into the newsroom. I caught a glimpse of a dozen staring faces before the door swung closed again.

I took her by the arm. "Come on," I growled. "Let's get out of here. Too much traffic."

She was more at home on a high stool in a bar, although climbing on to a high stool with that skirt was a complicated manoeuvre. Although it was morning, she asked for Scotch, took a long cigarette holder from her bag for the cigarette I gave her.

"You've remembered something about Sparman?" I asked.

"Yes, honey," she drawled. "After you'd gone, I got to thinking. There was one fella I remembered, a fella who was a friend of Sparman."

I tried to control my eagerness, leaned forward only slightly. "What was his name? Where can I find him?"

She drew languidly on the cigarette, ash fell from the end and drifted down on her. She took a tiny square of handkerchief from her pocket, fastidiously dabbed at the grey specks which marred creamy whiteness. I gulped. The over-spilling expanse of soft flesh seemed to throb with indignation at the unnaturally prominent position it had been forcibly moulded to occupy.

"You've left a spot there," I said.

"Where?"

"There!"

She dabbed some more. "Thanks, honey."

"This guy," I said. "His name and address?"

She fluttered her eyelids at me, inspected the hem of her skirt thoughtfully, gently scratched her knee with a pointed, blood-red nail. "What's in it for me?"

I sighed. "Ten bucks."

"I came here to see you special," she flared. "Took a long while making myself look respectable too. D'you think I work for peanuts?"

"What d'ya want?" I asked wearily.

"Fifty bucks."

I compromised at thirty bucks. She asked for it right away. I counted it out slowly in front of her. She took it from me, rolled it tightly, shot a quick glance around the bar and then tucked it away. I don't know what she used for a money box, but it was somewhere underneath her skirt. She smoothed her skirt over her thighs, smiled at me coyly. "If you wanna make it another five bucks, fella; look me up tonight and you can tuck it away yourself."

"I'll stick with the thirty bucks' worth," I said. "Who's the guy?"

She took a deep breath. "I'm not gonna say it's gonna do you much good," she confessed, safe in the knowledge my dough was tucked away. "I only knew Sparman a little while. During that time he stopped at a hotel called The Belvedere. He had a friend there, a man named Cohen. I saw Sparman with him a number of times."

"D'you remember what he looked like?"

She puckered her brow. "It's such a long while ago. I think he was kinda dark, middling build. I guess I can't remember much more."

"Give me the address of The Belvedere."

She gave it to me. I noted it carefully, offered to take her home. Her gay-nineties fashion would have gained attention in any bar in the world. Already she was being ogled and was ogling back.

"Don't worry about me, honey," she drawled. "You go right ahead. I guess I'll sit here quietly and have one more drink."

She wasn't lonely long. She had company ordering for her before I reached the exit. Once again she'd spilled ash, was

121

dabbing at it with a coy smile. The guy was looking at her like he was willing to tuck away every buck he owned.

* * *

The reception clerk at The Belvedere Hotel was a sleek, oily faced guy with an *I-know-everything* kinda smile.

But he didn't know Sparman. Had never heard of him.

"Let me talk to the manager," I growled.

He didn't like me and he didn't like my attitude. But there was something in my eyes which stopped him from arguing. He got the manager; a podgy little guy, with an oiled kiss-curl which stuck to his forehead like it was plastered there with margarine.

He was a guy with a memory. When I mentioned Sparman and recalled how he'd been killed by plunging over the cliff-top, he actually remembered him. It transpired he had reason to remember Sparman. The police had him in and out of the morgue a dozen times to get evidence of identification.

"There was a friend of Sparman's," I said. "He was stopping at the hotel the same time Sparman was here. A guy named Cohen."

He handed me an oily grin, nodded his head with vigour. "Sure," he said. "I remember Mr Cohen. I remember him good. He was a close friend of Mr Sparman."

I eyed him keenly. "It was four years ago. How come you remember him so clearly?"

He shrugged his shoulders, spread his hands. "Mr Cohen was so puzzling," he explained. "He was a friend of Mr Sparman's. Every meal they eat together. Then one day Mr Sparman went out, was killed. Mr Cohen went ahead of him. Mr Sparman wound up in the morgue and Mr Cohen never came back. Never came back at all."

"What about his things?" I asked quickly. "Did he take those with him?"

Again that expressive shrug of the shoulders and the spread hands. "He never paid his bill or nothing. Left his suitcase, left everything here."

"You still got that stuff?"

"D'you think I run my business for nothing?" he asked indignantly. "I hold that property. When Mr Cohen returns and pays, he will get back his suitcase."

I eyed him up and down. He was a Greek, a keen businessman. I said laconically: "Four years is a long time. How much did he owe?"

He eyed me up and down equally shrewdly. "Sixty bucks," he said quickly.

I took out my wallet, peeled off six ten-dollar bills. "Do I get to look at the luggage?"

He didn't argue. He tucked away the bills in his hip pocket, jerked his head for me to follow and led the way downstairs to the basement.

It was a storeroom. It looked like lots of guys left their luggage from time to time. Cohen's luggage was stowed away in a distant corner, musty and covered with dust. The manager snapped open the hasps of the suitcase, with fastidious fingers, dodged back as a swirl of dust arose.

I wasn't so lucky. I stepped in, threw open the suitcase lid and started to tumble the stuff out. It was the usual kinda stuff; shirts, socks, a coupla spare suits and other odds and ends. The only thing that interested me was a black leather wallet. There wasn't anything in it except a coupla dollar bills, an unusual ferry-boat ticket and a document proving Cohen was an able-bodied seaman.

That document was important. It was clean, folded neatly and looked as though it might have been used just once. I recovered it from the wallet, put it in my inside pocket.

The manager said: "I can have this stuff sent on for you."

"I don't need it," I told him. "I've got all I want." I took out my cigarette case, offered him a cigarette. As we lit up, I asked quietly: "How well do you remember this guy Cohen? Would you recognise him if you saw him?"

"It is a long while," he said doubtfully. "But I think so. I think I would recognise him."

I drew a photograph from my pocket, one I'd got from police headquarters. I showed it to him. "Ever seen this guy before?"

He looked at it. He didn't look at it very hard. "That's him," he said firmly. "That's Cohen right enough."

I sighed with relief. "Thanks a lot, pal, " I said. "Thanks a lot."

"For what?"

"For helping me get somewhere."

He just didn't understand; he looked at me blankly.

Cohen had disappeared the same night that Sparman had been killed. Sparman had been burnt beyond recognition in that smashed car. The manager had identified the photograph I had shown him.

That photograph was a blown-up reproduction from the police records. It was a photograph of Sparman the man who had been murdered.

It sure was interesting, and only one conclusion to be drawn. The manager had identified that photograph, claimed it was Cohen. So somehow, some time, Coen had become Sparman, completely assumed his identity.

123

It was information that was dynamite. But it still left a lotta questions to be answered. Why had Cohen assumed Sparman's identity? Was there any reason to believe Sparman's death had not been accidental but, instead, had been carefully arranged by Cohen?

And finally, the sixty-four dollar question had still to be answered. Why had Cohen - or Sparman, as he chose to call himself - been murdered?

CHAPTER THIRTEEN

I telephoned the office to see if anything was moving. The Chief had left a message he wanted to talk to me.

"How are you making out on the Sparman case?" he rasped.

"Getting places slowly," I told him. I was pleased with the progress I'd made but wanted to wait until I had it all tied in a neat parcel ready to drop in his lap before I let him in on anything.

"Got a new lead for you," he growled.

My heart fell. Maybe the police had got where I'd got.

"The cops found the murder weapon," he said. "I was tipped off about half an hour ago. Get round headquarters quick and you may learn something."

I caught a taxi to police headquarters, blustered my way through to the ballistics department. I wasn't the first to arrive. Jenny was waiting there, cross-legged and smoking a cigarette, out-staring a police sergeant who was acting like he'd never seen silk-sheathed legs before.

She turned her head, scowled up at me as I entered. Her lips twisted in a grim, cynical sneer. "Hiya, louse," she greeted.

"Hiya, Jenny," I said. My face was red. "I wish you'd give me a chance to explain ... how ..."

"Don't waste your breath," she drawled.

"But it wasn't intentional," I protested. "It was just that ..."

"Get lost," she rasped. "Knock off. Take a powder. Get out from under me."

"You're making a mistake, Jenny," I said quietly.

"I made two," she corrected. She smiled bitterly. "I deserved all I got."

"But I tell you Jenny, you made a mistake ..."

"I'll say," she snarled. "The first time a guy knifes you in the back, it's his fault. The second time he knifes you, it's your own fault."

"Don't be this way, Jenny," I pleaded. "You've got it ..."

A white-coated guy with horn-rimmed glasses opened the door, caught Jenny's eye, jerked his head as an invitation to enter. She got up quickly, clip-clopped across the room on her high-heels. I kept one pace behind her. She looked over her shoulder indignantly, handed me an icy stare. But it needed more than an icy stare to keep me away from anything of news value.

The white-coated guy knew Jenny. He knew me to. He pointed emotionlessly. "That's the murder gun," he said.

Jenny looked at it. I looked at it. "Can I pick it up?" she asked. "It don't bite," he told her.

She picked it up, examined it carefully. I looked over her shoulder, examined it with equal care. She flicked open the cartridge chamber, saw it was empty, closed it swiftly, spun around and triggered six non-existent slugs into the pit of my belly.

There were no explosions, no stabbing spurt of flame, no leaden slugs tearing through flesh. But the swift way she turned, the pointing muzzle and the sharp click of the hammer on empty cartridge chambers, turned my belly over. I worked up a weak smile. "Lucky it wasn't loaded."

Her eyes were angry, remembering her unjust treatment. "Too bad it wasn't loaded," she drawled. "It would have given you something to think about." Then her eyes and lips became mocking. "What's happened to the great he-man reporter? He's gone quite pale. Take a look at him, Ronny. He's gone quite white."

The white-overalled Ronny grinned. "What happened, Hank? She throw a scare into you?"

I let it ride. "Yeah," I croaked. "She threw a scare into me."

"Let's try it again, huh?" she said. She pointed the gun, triggered it some more. She pointed it just about the same way it musta been pointed at Sparman. My guts heeled over a second time. "It'd need six of the best like that to fix you," she said angrily.

I was trying to suppress the beating of my heart, kept my hands clenched tight and tried to swallow the lump in my throat. I asked in a kinda dried, stretched-out voice: "What about the bullets, Ronny? Do they match?"

"See for yourself," he invited. He motioned to the lighted screen that matched up the rifling inside a gun barrel with the scored marks on a used bullet.

There wasn't any doubt about it. They'd dug six slugs out of Sparman. They all matched the rifling on the gun exactly.

"Where did they dig up the gun?" I asked.

"Lonsdale Park," he said. "It'd been tossed in the boating pool. Wouldn't have been found for years if they hadn't decided to clean it out this week."

My mouth was dry. "Any prints found on the gun?"

"They got some," he said uninterestedly. "A bit smeared, but enough to give them a record."

"Have they checked?" I persisted. "Fingerprints belonging to a known criminal?"

He shook his head. "If they had, he'd have been sitting in a cell long before this."

Jenny was looking at me. One eyebrow was arched higher than the other. A question came into her eyes, an eager glint of

126

understanding. "You're on to something, Hank," she challenged. "You know something?"

I glowered at her. "Aw, you crazy dame," I jeered. "Always getting crazy ideas."

"You have!" she burst out triumphantly.

"You dunno what you're talking about," I contradicted gruffly. "I don't know a thing."

Her eyes were narrowed slits. "You've got something, Hank," she judged correctly. "And this time I'm gonna have it too. You've double-crossed me twice, played me for a sucker all along the line. This time I'm gonna stick to your coat-tails, let you do the digging while I get results."

"You're crazy," I said.

"I'd be even more crazy if I let you get out of my sight."

I stalked out of police headquarters. She kept right behind me. I took a coupla taxis. She tailed me tenaciously. I dropped into a bar, ordered a double Scotch. She came right into the bar after me, sat on the next stool, sipped a sherry and grinned mockingly.

"Cut it out, will ya, Jenny?" I pleaded. "I wanna fix up to see my girl. You know how it is; two's company, three's a crowd."

Her lips sneered. "You'll have to think up a better one than that."

I became desperate. "All right," I said. "I'll prove it."

She watched me while I shut myself in the telephone kiosk. I dialled Doris. When she answered, I said urgently: "Look, honey. Do me a favour will ya? Meet me for ten minutes."

"Something special, Hank?"

I tried to sound off-hand. "No. Nothing special. I'm at the Blenheim Bar. Could you drop in and see me for ten minutes?"

"Right now?"

"Soon as you can."

"All right," she agreed. "But I mustn't be any longer. Marion's got another headache. I don't like to leave her too long."

"Come right down, honey," I urged.

When she arrived, Jenny was sticking as close to me as my shadow. I waved to Doris as she appeared in the doorway, and as she came over, both of them were sizing each other up. There was a kinda saw-edge tension when I introduced them.

"What was it you wanted, honey," purred Doris.

I looked at Jenny. "This dame here," I sighed. "She's by way of being a business competitor. She figures it's her duty to stick on my tail. Now personally, I'm all in favour of an evening with you. But I'm all for a twosome. Jenny here wants to make it a threesome."

Doris stared at Jenny with wide eyes. "Well," she said with a surprised note in her voice. "If she feels that strongly about you, why doesn't she do something about it?"

I got out my silver cigarette case, noticed my engraved monogram didn't show up clearly, polished the silver case with my handkerchief.

"It's this way, honey," I said. "There's nothing between me and Jenny. She likes to think there is. She's been trying to build it into something really big and ..."

Jenny's eyes had been widening angrily as I spoke. When they'd widened to their uttermost, she burst out indignantly.

"Why of all the stupid, self-conceited, ignorant, self-opinionated ..."

I dropped my cigarette case. It hit the floor near Doris's foot, bounced twice and spilled cigarettes on the floor. I bent down quickly, cutting short Jenny's flow of criticism, and gathered up the cigarettes. Doris obligingly helped, picked up the cigarette case. I forgot about smoking, returned the case to my pocket. "I'm dreadfully sorry about this, honey," I told Doris. "You and me are due for a night out. But I just can't get rid of this vixen."

Jenny's eyes flashed dangerously. "Me! Vixen!"

I grinned easily. "Well, you just ain't gonna leave me alone, are you?"

She drew in a deep, angry breath, with an effort managed to say nothing. I flicked my eyes to Doris. "Look, honey," I said. "You and me wanna talk alone. We wanna have a little time together. So you toddle along home. I'll get in touch with you later. Okay?"

Doris looked mystified. She shook her head, smiling wryly. "I don't get any of it, Hank. It's all so crazy. Why do you have to see me? And does she really have to follow you around that way?"

I took her by the arm, squeezed her arm encouragingly. "Run along, honey," I urged. "I'll be in touch with you later. I'll give Queenie here the run-around, get in touch with you as soon as I've lost her."

Doris was still mystified. "Is this a game or something? What does it all mean? Do you always ..."

"Don't worry about it any more," I interrupted. "Jenny's a newspaper man the same as me. We're both crazy. Now run along, will ya, honey?"

Doris shrugged her shoulders, smiled when I winked at her encouragingly, nodded to Jenny and drifted out of the bar.

"How are you feeling?" I asked Jenny.

"Fine," she said. "How are you?"

"In the mood for action," I said. "You're gonna have to move fast to keep up with me. Boy, am I gonna give you the run-around."

"I don't think so," she smiled sweetly. She banged her glass on the counter to attract the bartender. "You give yourself the run-around," she invited. Then, as the bartender hovered, she pointed at me. "The gentleman wants the bill."

While I was still fumbling in my pocket, she was off like quicksilver, pushing through the swing-door, anxious to keep Doris in sight.

I sighed. Reporting's a bug. If you get it, you get it bad. And when you get it bad, there's a story in everything. A guy can't so much as pick up a spoon, without a newspaperman thinking there's something suspicious about it.

I'd lost Jenny. I'd have lost her sooner or later. She musta known it. Maybe that was why she decided to follow Doris, check up on her instead of trying to keep track of me.

I went back to police headquarters, went to the fingerprint department. Most of the guys there knew me well. It was lunchtime and only a coupla dicks were on duty. They were at the far end of the room, filing and indexing. I browsed around, toyed with some of the equipment they used. They knew me well enough to leave me alone, let me amuse myself.

I like playing around and experimenting. I'd spent hours in that fingerprint room, knew all the processes, understood how to operate all the expensive and intricate machinery they used. While those two dicks got on with their filing, I toyed with fingerprint equipment, experimented, utilised their camera, and finally drifted down towards them, holding a still damp negative in my fingers.

"What you got there?" asked one.

"Just playing around," I said mildly. "Blow it up for me, will ya? I wanna see what it looks like." I grinned derisively. "One of these days I'll apply for a job here, get one of you guys out on the street."

They grinned good-humouredly, took the negative from me, blew it up about twenty times its normal size, and projected it onto a white screen.

I studied it thoughtfully. They studied it too. I smiled proudly. "I figure that's a nice set of prints," I said.

"Yeah, not bad," one agreed reluctantly.

"Thanks," I said. "That's enough. I'll keep the negative as a memento."

The first one moved to switch it off. The second guy said with a keen, whiplash note in his voice: "Hold it a minute."

There was a kinda tenseness in the atmosphere, as he crossed the room, dug out another negative from a pigeonhole, came back to the machine, inserted it and projected it alongside the one already showing.

All three of us stared at the two prints. There was a long, long silence. The second guy rapped in a low, crisp voice: "Okay, Hank. Where d'ya get it?"

I gulped. Even a doll with three blind eyes could see that those two sets of fingerprints were identical. I countered his question with another. "Where did *you* get it?"

He switched off the apparatus, stared at me grimly. "Okay, Hank," he said firmly. "You've had your fun. Now stop kidding. Where did you get those prints we've just blown up?"

I worked up a chuckle. "Hey, what's happened to you guys? Why so serious?"

"I'm not kidding, Hank," he said grimly. "This is mighty important. Where did you get those prints?"

I swallowed, I gulped. My mind was racing madly. I took a deep breath and began to chuckle low down in my chest. He stared at me. He didn't think it funny.

"Okay, fellas," I chuckled. "Just my little joke. Skip it."

"What d'ya mean? Skip it. Where d'ya get those prints?"

I eyed him with mock solemnness, said in an artificial Brooklyn accent: "Okay, fellas. I come clean. When you weren't looking I swiped the negative out of the pigeonhole, duplicated it. Then I put the original negative back, asked you to blow this up and waited to see what would happen."

He glared. Then his face softened. He began to chuckle. "Aw, you sure fooled me on that one. Hanged if I saw you go anywhere near that pigeonhole."

"Got you pretty worked up, didn't it?"

"It sure did, fella." He grinned wryly. "The moment I saw it, I knew I'd seen it before. As soon as I checked, I thought I was on to something."

"On to something?" I looked deliberately blank.

"You know what those prints are?"

"No?" I said. I tried to look mystified. It was working out better than I'd hoped and worse than I'd hoped.

"Those prints come from the gun that killed Sparman," he said. "You can understand how keen I was to know where you'd got them."

"Is that where they came from?" I gasped, tried to look a little shocked. Deep down inside I was shocked. If it hadn't worked out this way, I'd intended asking him to show me those prints. And now I'd seen them anyway, I wasn't happy about it.

"That was pretty smart, Joe," I said. "Millions of fingerprints, every one different, and yet you remembered those particular ones so well."

He smiled embarrassedly, inwardly proud of himself but trying to be modest. "It isn't that difficult," he said. "You get to know the formation of the whorls, and I've been working on that set today. They were fresh in my mind."

"Just the same," I said. "I figure it was pretty smart work. I'll speak to the Commissioner about you, maybe get you a rise."

It was light-hearted banter. But I was sick inside, and got out of there as quick as I could, walked around with my mind turning over and over, wound up outside Sparman's apartment.

I was remembering it all over again now. Sparman's agonised face, his bullet-mutilated body, the fact he was really Cohen, a merchant seaman who had changed places with Sparman and assumed his identity. Add to that the fact that Sparman kept himself to himself, worked his way into an important job in an atomic engine manufacturing company and frequented a German restaurant.

It was all churning over and over in my mind. Again I was walking, blindly, not realising where I was going. Then I suddenly did realise. I was passing through Lonsdale Park, passing the pond where the gun had been found. It was still being cleaned out. I realised in the same moment that the park was halfway between Sparman's apartment and where Doris lived.

I wasn't expected, but that didn't worry me. I went up to Doris's apartment, thumbed the bell and felt even sicker inside.

She opened up, smiled at me with quick relief and widened the door. "Just in time for tea," she said brightly.

I threw my hat on a chair, sank down wearily on the settee. "I don't want any tea."

"But you must. I'm in the middle of making it. It won't take a minute."

"Doris!" I said commandingly.

She turned and stared at me, surprised by the harshness of my voice. Her eyes were a large question mark.

I jerked my head towards the bedroom door. "Where's Marion? In there?"

"Asleep," she said. "I don't want to disturb her." She nodded towards a corner where an array of new suitcases were neatly lined up and labelled. "We're leaving tonight for Florida. We have our air passages booked. I want to take her away, give her a long rest."

"I've been busy," I said. "I've been checking all day. I found out things."

"What things, Hank?" Her eyes were troubled now.

"About Sparman," I said. "His name wasn't Sparman. His name was Cohen. He was a merchant seaman."

There was a kinda rigidity about her now. "And ...?" she said.

"The cops found the murder gun," I said.

There was a long pause. A very long pause. She said faintly: "What about it, Hank? Why are you acting this way?"

"I've seen the murder gun," I repeated heavily. "I recognised it."

She gave a kinda gasp. Her eyes were wide now and frightened. I couldn't bear to look at her. I stared in front of me, went on talking slowly. "The murder gun was the gun Marion kept in the bedside table."

"You're crazy, Hank," she said in a whisper. "You don't know what you're talking about."

"Would you care to show me Marion's gun?"

There was another long silence. "I've lost it," she said, so softly I hardly heard her.

"A few more things," I went on. "The gun was thrown in the lake in Lonsdale Park. The Park's open all night. Anybody walking from Sparman's flat to this apartment could take a direct line through the Park, drop the gun in the lake as they passed through."

There was another long pause. "What are you trying to say, Hank?" she asked hoarsely.

"I'm not trying to say anything," I rasped. "I'm just stating facts. Fingerprints have been checked. There were fingerprints on the murder gun. They're identical to the fingerprints I collected on my cigarette case when you picked it up."

I looked at her then. She didn't look guilty. She looked hunted, worried. She moistened her lips with the tip of her tongue. "Then ... the police know?"

The sentence was almost a confession. I felt so sick I had to clench my teeth tightly before I could speak. "The police don't know ... yet! I handled the fingerprints myself, blew up the prints on the cigarette case, compared them with the prints on the gun."

She got up, crossed to the window and stood staring out. She stood that way for several minutes without saying a word. I got up slowly, reached for my hat. She spun round, faced me with a kinda glaring challenge in her eyes.

"What are you going to do?" she demanded.

I crammed my hat on my head. I was sick inside and suddenly angry at all of it. So sick and angry I wanted to destroy things. "What the hell d'you think I'm going to do?" I flared.

"You're going to the police then?" she said quietly.

I lit a cigarette, stood staring at her. "You're a good guesser."

132

"Listen, Hank," she pleaded. "We're going away tonight. Our luggage is packed. We can go to Florida. Nobody will ever know anything about it. It all depends on ... you!"

I was angry again, burning inside. I flung my cigarette on the floor, ground it into the carpet savagely. "D'you think I want to do it?" I demanded. "D'you think I want to send you to the hot-squat? But this is a civilised country. Folks just can't go around shooting men, wilfully, brutally and painfully."

"You mustn't say anything, Hank," she whispered. "It'd be so easy. You could forget all about it."

"Jeepers. Are you crazy? D'you think I could ever forget it?"

"It was so understandable," she said softly. "It was really ... justice!"

All my angry emotions had kinda burnt out now, seeped away, leaving me just a worn-out shell. But I knew what I had to do. "I'm sorry, Doris," I said quietly. "I don't know the how or the whyfor of it. But you killed him. That's all I have to know."

Her eyes widened with surprise. "Hank! You don't think *I* killed him!"

I raised my eyes to heaven. "Jeepers!" I said.

"But I didn't, Hank," she protested fiercely. "I didn't kill him. I thought you understood. I thought you knew everything."

"What is there to know?" I asked wearily.

"You thought it was *me* who killed him and not Mar ..." She broke off abruptly, pressed her lips tightly together. I was on her in two quick strides, grasping her by the wrists.

"What were you going to say?" I rasped. "You were gonna say Marion killed him. Well, maybe she did. That makes two of you together. She killed him and you helped. Heaven knows why. But that makes a pair of you going in the chair. What's the matter with you both? Are you crazy?"

"Marion was," she said quietly. She twisted her wrists free from my hands, stared at me defiantly. "Tell them if you like, Hank. But it won't make any difference. You'll just cause Marion more suffering. Unnecessary suffering. She's gone through so much already. Why are you making it worse?"

My head was going round in circles. This was murder. A human, living man, with the spark of life deliberately extinguished. Life is important. You might almost say it's holy. But Doris didn't seem to have that angle. She seemed to figure it was right to kill the guy. Maybe she and Marion had seen so much suffering and so many deaths in that concentration camp they'd become immune to the finer values of life.

"I've gotta do it," I said quietly. "Don't you see that, Doris? I've gotta do it."

Her eyes were dull, despairing. "All so unnecessary," she said. "All so unnecessary."

"She didn't have to kill him," I rasped. "Why the hell did she do it anyway?"

Her eyes switched to mine. "She had to," she said simply. "She couldn't help herself. She killed him and came back here with the gun. I took it out, threw it in the pond."

"Why did she have to kill him?" I persisted.

"His name wasn't Sparman," she said bleakly.

"I know it wasn't," I gritted. "His name was Cohen. A merchant seaman."

A wry smile twisted her lips. "His name wasn't Cohen either," she said. "Somehow he must have escaped from Europe, obtained false papers, shipped himself over to this country and got himself a job where he could learn things that might be of value to him later."

I eyed her narrowly. "You knew him, then?" I said. My mind raced. I remembered how Marion had fainted when she'd first seen Sparman at the car demonstration. "You knew him," I said again. "Marion knew him. That's why she fainted when she saw him ..." I broke off. A half-idea was forming at the back of my mind, but I was rejecting it as it formed.

It was as though Doris was reading my mind. "You know who he was!"

"You mean it was ..." I licked my lips. "No, it couldn't be," I protested. "Sparman was a chubby little guy, dark haired and with a moustache."

"Sparman was Schutz," she said quietly.

"But ..." I protested. "You said Schutz was tall, fair, had black eyes."

"Sparman was Schutz," she repeated. "I started to tell you about the camp before Schutz was killed. Afterwards ..." she shrugged her shoulders. "Afterwards, there was nothing I could do. I had to go on telling you, so I altered my description of Schutz."

I sat down, mopped my forehead. Everything was suddenly becoming very different. It all added up now. Schutz escaping from Germany, working his way over to America with a ticket as a merchant seaman, developing a friendship with the real Sparman who had no friends and relatives, somehow arranging an accident so he could take over Sparman's identity, become an American citizen with an identity number, a background, and the credit of being in the American Army. Yeah, the more I thought about it, the more it added together. Naturally, Schutz would get a job where he could learn about atomic engineering. These fascists were fanatical. The hope that fascism would one day be revived was strong inside them.

And what of Marion? The last time she'd seen Schutz had been in the concentration camp before her mind became a blank. He'd been transferred before she recovered from that shock. Then the other day she'd seen him, come face to face with him.

It was murder. In any court of America it was murder. I don't know the state of Marion's mind when she shot Schutz, but she'd inflicted on him just retribution not only for her own suffering, but for the suffering of thousands of other women in that far away camp of misery.

Doris looked at me pleadingly. "I could take her away, Hank," she said. "Nobody need ever know. Marion's getting better now. It's like she's got rid of something that was inside her. Something that was poisoning her."

I got up, fumbled in my pocket for another cigarette. I lit it slowly, kept staring at her the whole time. It was all different now. Sure, it was murder. But you could only call it that by sticking to the letter of the law. I remembered the way I'd felt about Schutz when Doris had described to me what had happened. I remembered how I'd sat listening to her, sweating and burning to wrap my fingers around his neck.

"It's not so terrible, Hank," she pleaded. "It happened everywhere in Europe after the liberation. The people took the law into their own hands, hunted down the oppressors, executed them"

I drew on my cigarette. She was still staring at me, eyes pleading. The luggage was ready and waiting and I could see the air tickets in an envelope on the mantelpiece. In a matter of hours they'd be on their way to Florida. It all depended on me.

The bedroom door opened unexpectedly. Startled, I turned towards it. Marion was framed in the doorway. She was wearing a blood-red negligee, her face still white and drawn. But now I looked closely I could see there was something about her that was different. It was as though she'd found something inside herself, found something to live for. She looked at me, nodded slightly. She said to Doris: "Are you gonna make some tea?"

"Aw, yes, honey; I clean forgot about it. Hank here ..."

"Hiya, Marion," I said.

She worked up a weak smile. "Hiya," she said. It was the first sign of human feeling I'd seen in her. I could imagine her in Florida, drinking in the sun, turning her white cheeks brown, and daily becoming more rested and healthy.

"I'll be getting along," I said.

I nodded to them both, had my hand on the door handle when Doris called sharply: "Hank!"

I turned around. She was staring at me with a question in her eyes. I looked at Marion. I said: "Have a nice time in Florida, honey." I looked back at Doris. "Look me up when you're in town again."

Her eyes were moist with tears of thankfulness. "I will, Hank," she said fervently. "I will."

I closed the door of their apartment behind me, peered across the corridor at Jenny, who was propping up the wall opposite. She smiled at me sweetly. "You forgot to tell me there were two girl friends," she said.

I scowled, strode along the corridor. She clip-clopped along beside me, shared the lift down with me, kept at my side as we left the apartment.

"If you honestly feel this way about me, Jenny," I told her, "I'll drop those two dames. The way I figure it, you're equal to two of them at any time."

"Don't get ideas, wolf," she retorted. "You know why I'm sticking to you. You're on to something," she insisted. "You can't fool me. I know you're on to it. I'm gonna stick close, get as much out of it as you do."

I sighed. "Okay," I said. "I'll make a compromise. We'll work this together. We'll be partners. How's that?"

She stared at me strangely. "I'll accept on sufferance. Where do we start?"

"We start some place I can eat," I said. "I'm hungry."

Her eyes were narrow slits. "I can stick to you easier when we're not crowded. I've got an ice-box at my flat. I can fix up a meal."

I smiled broadly. "That's real fine. There's nothing I'd like better. And afterwards ..."

"Afterwards," she said firmly, "we get on with the job."

"What job?"

She eyed me reprovingly. "You know damned well what job."

"Okay," I sighed.

We took a taxi to her apartment. I'd visited her before, knew she had two telephones. For that reason, I stopped in the lobby, made a call from a public kiosk. She waited outside, tapping one heel impatiently, convinced I was manoeuvring to give her the slip.

"That you Chief," I said into the phone.

"What d'ya want?" he growled. "I'm busy."

"I've got competition in my hair," I said. "You can help me. When I ring up later ..."

"Who were you phoning?," she asked suspiciously when I came out.

I looked mysterious, sheepish, acted embarrassed. "Aw, just a guy I know."

Her eyes glinted. "We're partners," she pointed out. "No double-crossing."

"On the level, honey," I said. "On the level."

Jenny was smart all ways. She was a smart dresser, a smart looker, a tenacious newspaper woman, and in a short while she threw together a meal that was delicious and satisfying. She kept trying to pump me on what I knew, and I kept evading her questions. From time to time, I furtively consulted my wristwatch. Finally I couldn't bear the strain any longer. "Look, honey," I said. "I've gotta make a call. Okay?"

"Help yourself," she said, indicating the telephone.

I flushed, shuffled my feet. "It's kinda personal," I said. "It's a dame I had a date with and ..." I flushed even more.

"Okay, Hank," she said with sweet artfulness. "I'll leave you to it."

She swayed off into the bedroom, discreetly closing the door behind her. She'd probably forgotten I knew she had an extension telephone in her bedroom.

I picked up the receiver, listened and heard the faint click that came when she picked up her receiver. I dialled the office, got through to the Chief.

"It's Hank here," I whispered hoarsely.

"Can you talk?"

"It's difficult," I said. "Did you get it?"

"Got it just this minute. You're right all the way along the line. The guy's name is Ransom. Seventeen Meadow Avenue, Ruston. It'll take you a coupla hours in a fast car to get there. Everything checks perfectly. So get there quick, somehow get a set of his prints and then everything's in the bag."

"Leave it to me, Chief," I said. "I'll be ringing later."

I replaced the receiver, switched on an unconcerned smile, walked across to the bedroom and knocked on the door. She took a long time opening up, stared at me with a far-too-innocent expression. "Are you through phoning now, honey?"

"Yeah," I said indifferently. "She thought I was trying to give her the brush-off. But I squared it." I looked at my watch furtively, glanced longingly at my hat.

"Well," she said brightly. "Where do we start?"

I looked at my watch again. "Look, Jenny," I said. "I've had a long day. What say we skip it for tonight, huh?"

Her wide eyes were anxious for me. "Of course, Hank," she said. "You're tired, aren't you?" She came close, fingered my forehead.

"What makes?" I growled.

"You been around the machines today?"

"Nope."

"How come you got printer's ink smeared all over your forehead?"

I rubbed at it with my handkerchief. The handkerchief came away clean. "It's dried, dear," she said. "You'd better wash it off." She nodded. "You know the bathroom."

I knew where the bathroom was right enough. I looked in the mirror, couldn't see any printer's ink. I combed my hair, washed my hands and gave two hefty tugs at the door before I realised Jenny had discreetly locked it from the outside.

I hammered the panels, kept hammering. But the door was stout. A little later, her mocking voice sounded. "Are you there, honey?"

"Where in hell can I go?," I demanded indignantly. "Open this door."

"Aw, honey," she cooed. "Have you got locked in the powder room?"

My heart sank. I gulped, rattled the door-knob, hammered the panels with my fists. "Open up, you little minx," I yelled. "Open up, you damned double-crosser."

"Don't be impatient, honey," she cooed. "I'll be back."

"Open up," I roared.

"I'll bring a paper with me," she mocked. "You can read all about what happened at Ruston."

I heard the door of her flat slam and sat on the edge of the bath disconsolately. I sighed. I sure had been taken for a sucker. I'd been just a little too clever. Sending Jenny to Ruston on a wild-goose chase was one thing, getting myself locked in the bathroom until she got back wasn't so funny.

I looked at my watch. It was ten minutes to take-off time. In just ten minutes, Doris and Marion would be safely on their way to Florida, on their way to starting a new life. I sighed. It had been a lotta worry, a lotta trouble and it got me nowhere. I couldn't even use enough of the story to fill a coupla paragraphs.

I was gonna miss Doris. She was a nice dame and I'd just been getting to know her. I shook my head woefully. I could have worked up a lotta steam over that girl.

I got up, tried the window, tried the door. I could get out by busting the door. I didn't wanna do that. I didn't wanna smash up Jenny's flat. She sure had taken me for a sucker. I grinned ruefully. I had four long, cold, dreary hours before me. But I had to hand it to Jenny. She'd got back on me in style. She'd have scooped me neatly, too, if there really had been a guy at Ruston.

I took out a cigarette, lit up thoughtfully, reconciled myself to my long wait. There were compensations in everything. I'd worked hard and got no story. I'd got worked up over Doris and finally lost her.

But there were compensations. Jenny had been mad at me because I'd ditched her on two important occasions. Now she'd ditched me. She'd figured it had evened things up. Even if she did come back tired from a wild-goose chase, she'd still figure she was even with me.

Sitting there in that pokey bathroom, perched on the edge of the tub, I even began to feel a little happy.

Yeah, when Jenny came back tired, she'd be happy about one thing. She'd be happy about catching me napping. And I didn't mind. Because if Jenny came back happy, that was okay by me. Because Jenny was a warm-hearted, warm-natured dame, and when she got back it would be late. Too late for the night buses.

I had the certain feeling Jenny wouldn't send me out into the cold, cold night to walk myself home.

OTHER TITLES FROM TELOS PUBLISHING

DOCTOR WHO

DOCTOR WHO: TIME AND RELATIVE by Kim Newman
The harsh British winter of 1962/3 brings a big freeze and with it comes a new, far greater menace: terrifying icy creatures are stalking the streets, bringing death and destruction.
An adventure featuring the first Doctor and Susan.
Featuring a foreword by Justin Richards.
Deluxe edition frontispiece by Bryan Talbot.
£10 (+ £1.50 UK p&p) Standard h/b ISBN: 1-903889-02-2
£25 (+ £1.50 UK p&p) Deluxe h/b ISBN: 1-903889-03-0

DOCTOR WHO: CITADEL OF DREAMS by Dave Stone
In the city-state of Hokesh, time plays tricks; the present is unreliable, the future impossible to intimate.
An adventure featuring the seventh Doctor and Ace.
Featuring a foreword by Andrew Cartmel.
Deluxe edition frontispiece by Lee Sullivan.
£10 (+ £1.50 UK p&p) Standard h/b ISBN: 1-903889-04-9
£25 (+ £1.50 UK p&p) Deluxe h/b ISBN: 1-903889-05-7

DOCTOR WHO: NIGHTDREAMERS by Tom Arden
Perihelion Night on the wooded moon Verd. A time of strange sightings, ghosts, and celebration. But what of the mysterious and terrifying Nightdreamers? And of the Nightdreamer King?
An adventure featuring the third Doctor and Jo.
Featuring a foreword by Katy Manning.
Deluxe edition frontispiece by Martin McKenna.
£10 (+ £1.50 UK p&p) Standard h/b ISBN: 1-903889-06-5
£25 (+ £1.50 UK p&p) Deluxe h/b ISBN: 1-903889-07-3

DOCTOR WHO: GHOST SHIP by KeithTopping
The TARDIS lands in the most haunted place on Earth, the luxury ocean liner the Queen Mary on its way from Southampton to New York in the year 1963. But why do ghosts from the past, the present and, perhaps even the future, seek out the Doctor?
An adventure featuring the fourth Doctor.
Featuring a foreword by Hugh Lamb.
Deluxe edition frontispiece by Dariusz Jasiczak.
SOLD OUT Standard h/b ISBN: 1-903889-08-1
SOLD OUT Deluxe h/b ISBN: 1-903889-09-X

DOCTOR WHO: FOREIGN DEVILS by Andrew Cartmel

The Doctor, Jamie and Zoe find themselves joining forces with a psychic investigator named Carnacki to solve a series of strange murders in an English country house.
An adventure featuring the second Doctor, Jamie and Zoe.
Featuring a foreword by Mike Ashley.
Deluxe edition frontispiece by Mike Collins.
SOLD OUT Standard h/b ISBN: 1-903889-10-3
£25 (+ £1.50 UK p&p) Deluxe h/b ISBN: 1-903889-11-1

DOCTOR WHO: RIP TIDE by Louise Cooper

Strange things are afoot in a sleepy Cornish village. Could they have anything to do with the mysteriously beautiful Ruth, whom local lifeboatman Steve has taken a shine to… or could the other stranger, a man calling himself the Doctor be somehow involved?
An adventure featuring the eighth Doctor.
Featuring a foreword by Stephen Gallagher.
Deluxe edition frontispiece by Fred Gambino.
£10 (+ £1.50 UK p&p) Standard h/b ISBN: 1-903889-12-X
£25 (+ £1.50 UK p&p) Deluxe h/b ISBN: 1-903889-13-8

DOCTOR WHO: WONDERLAND by Mark Chadbourn

San Francisco 1967. Summer has lost her boyfriend, and fears him dead, destroyed by a new drug nicknamed Blue Moonbeams. Her only friends are three English tourists: Ben and Polly, and the mysterious Doctor. But will any of them help Summer, and what is the strange threat posed by the Blue Moonbeams?
An adventure featuring the second Doctor, Ben and Polly.
Featuring a foreword by Graham Joyce.
Deluxe edition frontispiece by Dominic Harman.
£10 (+ £1.50 UK p&p) Standard h/b ISBN: 1-903889-14-6
£25 (+ £1.50 UK p&p) Deluxe h/b ISBN: 1-903889-15-4

FICTION

URBAN GOTHIC: LACUNA & OTHER TRIPS
ed. David J. Howe
Stories by Graham Masterton, Christopher Fowler, Simon Clark, Debbie Bennett, Paul Finch, Steve Lockley & Paul Lewis.
Based on the Channel 5 horror series.
SOLD OUT ISBN: 1-903889-00-6 signed and numbered paperback

THE MANITOU by Graham Masterton
A 25th Anniversary author's preferred edition of this classic horror novel. An ancient Red Indian medicine man is reincarnated in modern day New York intent on reclaiming his land from the white men.
£9.99 (+ £1.50 p&p) ISBN: 1-903889-70-7 paperback
£30.00 (+ £2.50 p&p) ISBN: 1-903889-71-5 signed and numbered hardback

CAPE WRATH by Paul Finch
Death and horror on a deserted Scottish island as an ancient Viking warrior chief returns to life.
£8.00 (+ £1.50 p&p) ISBN: 1-903889-60-X

TELEVISION GUIDES

BEYOND THE GATE: THE UNOFFICIAL AND UNAUTHORISED GUIDE TO *STARGATE SG-1*
by Keith Topping
Complete episode guide to the popular TV show.
£9.99 (+ £2.50 p&p) ISBN: 1-903889-50-2

A DAY IN THE LIFE: THE UNOFFICIAL AND UNAUTHORISED GUIDE TO *24* by KEITH TOPPING
Complete episode guide to season 1 of the popular TV show.
£9.99 (+ £2.50 p&p) ISBN: 1-903889-53-7

The prices shown are correct at time of going to press. However, the publishers reserve the right to increase prices from those previously advertised without prior notice.

TELOS PUBLISHING
c/o Beech House
Chapel Lane
Moulton
Cheshire
CW9 8PQ
Email: orders@telos.co.uk
Web: www.telos.co.uk

To order copies of any Telos books, please visit our website where there are full details of all titles and facilities for worldwide credit card online ordering, or send a cheque or postal order (UK only) for the appropriate amount (including postage and packing), together with details of the book(s) you require, plus your name and address to the above address. Overseas readers please send two international reply coupons for details of prices and postage rates.